bad boys

After Dark

–Carson–

EVERYTHING'S NAUGHTIER AFTER DARK...

Billionaires After Dark Series

Melissa Foster

ISBN-13: 978-1-941480-68-7
ISBN-10: 1-941480-68-3

BAD BOYS AFTER DARK: CARSON

Cover Design: Elizabeth Mackey Designs

WORLD LITERARY PRESS
PRINTED IN THE UNITED STATES OF AMERICA

A Note to Readers

I am so excited to bring you Carson and Tawny's story. Carson has been the most mysterious of the Bad brothers since the day I met him two years ago, and now I know why. I hope you fall as hard for him and Tawny as I did.

You'll find previews of more upcoming publications at the end of their story, but the best way to keep up to date with releases is to sign up for my newsletter. Plus, you'll receive a free short story just for signing up.
www.melissafoster.com/newsletter

—Download free Love in Bloom ebooks:
www.melissafoster.com/LIBFree

—Download free reader goodies including family trees, series order, and more:
www.melissafoster.com/RG

Melissa Foster

For Sharon

Chapter One

IT WAS HIS kiss, his touch, and the promise of so much more in his rich cocoa eyes that had taunted Tawny Bishop in the wee hours of the night for the past decade and had finally driven her from Paris to New York City on this cold November night. Memories of her once best friend's demanding hands running over her heated flesh, enticing her into giving him anything he wanted, brought a rush of adrenaline, and her nerves flamed to life. A cacophony of wind and rain created a dark serenade to her seductive and nerve-racking thoughts as the cab weaved through traffic toward the Ultimate Hotel, where his family was hosting a fundraiser.

Carson Bad.

Even his name sounded stable and strong. She felt a smile tugging at her lips. *You were bad, all right.* His friendship and his deep, confident voice had once been the salve to all of her worries, righting everything that had felt wrong during her college years. God, she missed him. One sinful Sunday night his voice had done more than soothe. It had slithered beneath her skin, fueling her desires, and he'd introduced her to his darker, sensual side. *Look at me, Tawny. What do you see?* Her pulse quickened with the memory of him perched above her, her arms bound with silk above her head, his body bearing deliciously down on her. *You, Carson. I see you*, she'd answered. It hadn't been enough of an answer. She'd known it then, and it had haunted her in the years since. But she'd been too entranced, so turned on for the first time in her life, rational thinking had not been an option. And every Sunday night for almost two years thereafter, their connection had deepened as they'd explored their sexuality, testing boundaries and taking their fill like drunks at an exclusive bar. Those dark desires had consumed her, making it hard for her to concentrate on anything else. Shame had topped that sexual sundae, making their secret pleasures guilt-inducing and alienating. Until one fateful night when a knock had sounded on his apartment door, and Tawny's brilliant, lust-addled brain had kicked into gear—and her heart had taken a hit.

She'd been thinking rationally ever since, and as it turned out, a decade of rational thinking was not all it was cracked up to be. Their initial sexual encounter had been the first time meticulously careful and private Tawny had acted on a whim. Coming to see Carson was the second. She'd seen the announcement for the fundraiser only three days earlier, and had been a nervous wreck ever since making her flight arrangements.

She stared out at the dark, rainy night, thinking about her father, who had passed away two years ago from pancreatic cancer. Her mother had been killed while crossing the street when Tawny was only five years old, and her father had never remarried. Days before his death, her father had asked Tawny one question that had changed the direction of her life. Did she have any regrets? That simple question had spurred a torrent of emotions and was the catalyst for her divorce, her move to Paris, and her need to finally deal with her feelings for Carson.

"Ma'am?"

The cabdriver's irritated tone tore her from her thoughts.

She must have zoned out, which was no surprise after the excruciating delays on her almost nine-hour flight, during which she was seated next to a man who smelled like garlic and body odor. She paid the driver, slung her bag over her shoulder, and stepped out of the cab. A brisk gust of wind stung her cheeks as the driver lifted her suitcase from the trunk. She pulled her cashmere peacoat tight around her and thanked the doorman for helping her with her suitcase as she entered the hotel.

Happy to be out of the bitter cold, and beyond nervous about seeing Carson, Tawny was still in a state of shock that she was actually there. She drew in a deep, calming breath, inhaling the soft, warm scent of figs, the hottest trend in fragrances. Many upscale hotels and businesses had begun pumping in the aroma to elicit warm, homey feelings for their customers. As a perfumer, Tawny noticed, and distinguished, scents first, using them like DNA to get a read on people and places. Fig was nice, but it was not the scent she was seeking.

Her pulse hammered like thunder in her ears as she zeroed in on the sign announcing Carson's family's annual fundraiser. In the center of the sign was a picture of Lorelei Bad, his younger sister, who had passed away from leukemia when she was only eight years old. She wondered if Carson had been sad tonight, or if the event had been cathartic for him.

A hotel staff member appeared from behind the sign. He lifted it from its easel and walked down a hallway. *No!* She couldn't be too late. Not after getting up the nerve to finally come see Carson to try to figure out how to move on with her life.

Pulling her suitcase behind her, she ran across the marble floor. She didn't care if she was perspiring from nerves and probably looked as fatigued as she felt. She had to see Carson before she lost her courage. "Wait! Please!"

The man turned, exhaustion written in the dark circles beneath his eyes. A practiced smile lifted his lips. "Yes?"

"The fundraiser? Which suite is it in?" She sounded as breathless as she felt.

His smile faded, and her heart sank.

"I'm sorry, but it's over. It was in the Grand Ballroom, right through those doors." He pointed down the hall.

"Thank you." She hurried down the hall and burst through the doors, stumbling to a stop in the nearly empty room. Hotel staff were clearing away tables and chairs, along with the remnants of what looked like a beach-themed event. Pictures of young children lined the walls. Children who she assumed had fallen prey to leukemia, too, making the discovery of the vacant room feel that much sadder.

Her phone vibrated in her bag. Knowing it was probably her ex-husband, Keith, making sure she'd arrived safely, she let it go to voicemail. She didn't need her oh so patient ex trying to make her feel better.

She couldn't have asked for a more amicable divorce, especially given that during their marriage Keith had felt Carson's presence like a barrier between them just as strongly as she had. And he'd known exactly whom she was thinking about. She wasn't sure she would have been as understanding as Keith, but they'd managed to remain friends. Unfortunately, he'd never let her go completely. At first she had allowed his constant calls and texts to continue after they were divorced because it had been comforting to know someone was watching out for her when she'd moved to Paris. Only Keith had begun to take it too far, keeping tabs on her as though she couldn't take care of herself, and it was becoming a problem. She'd spent the last two years trying to figure out who she was, and Keith didn't have that answer. She'd never been her true self with him.

There was only one man who knew her better than she knew herself—and by the looks of the empty ballroom, she'd missed him.

This is why I shouldn't ever do things on a whim, she told herself as she lugged her suitcase toward the lobby. She knew better than to jet across the Atlantic unannounced. What if Carson was married? Or if he didn't even remember her? Had she been the type of study partner and lover who had gotten lost in a long line of willing women? She'd convinced herself that their relationship was unforgettable, one of a kind. *Maybe even true love.* If the spark was still there, and she hadn't blown it out of proportion after all these years, then maybe they had a chance for something real after all. And what if she couldn't tell how strong the spark was? What if there was *no* spark? Thinking there was no spark and believing it were two different things. *Oh God!* She was too confused. How could she move forward with her life unless she knew exactly where they stood?

Carson was a private man, with no social media profiles or public listings of his address or phone number. They were similar in that way, though for different reasons, and it was one of the many things she adored about him. The only way to see him now was to muster the courage to visit him at his office, which she knew she wouldn't do. It was one thing to embarrass herself at a public event where she could slip out unnoticed if he was accompanied by a woman. *A wife?* Her stomach knotted with the thought. It was quite another thing to be asked a million questions by an assistant about why she didn't have an appointment. Not to mention she would be taking the risk of

Carson telling an assistant he didn't want to see her.

Oh Lord. This really was a stupid idea.

"Welcome to the Ultimate Hotel," said the all-too-perky brunette behind the reception desk. "How may I help you?"

Get me on a plane back to Paris, stat. "I'd like a room for the night, please."

The woman's expression softened. "I'm sorry, but there are several events in town this weekend, and we are completely sold-out."

Are you kidding me? "Thank you. What is the closest hotel?"

"I'm afraid you'll have a tough time finding a room anywhere nearby on such short notice this weekend, but"—she pulled a piece of paper from a drawer—"you can try these hotels."

Tawny glanced at the paper, wishing she hadn't sold her father's house. At least then she'd have a place to stay. But she'd been too overcome with grief to think she'd ever want to step foot in it again. "Thank you."

She stepped to the side and looked over the list of hotels. An intoxicating, familiar aroma filtered into her senses. She closed her eyes, silently dissecting it with each inhalation. Moroccan tangerine, juniper leaves, champagne, lavender, sandalwood, and if she wasn't mistaken—*which she never was*—amber and rum, with an underlying uniqueness that only one man had ever possessed.

Carson.

The scent traveled inside her, winding around memories of their college years and gathering them like fish in a net. One after another they peppered her mind. Carson's smiles over textbooks, the gentle nudge of his shoulder, the push of his finger along her cheek as he tucked her hair behind her ear after hours of studying. His deep laughter and witty comments as they watched their favorite sci-fi shows whispered through her head. With her heart in her throat, she lifted her gaze, and lost her breath at the sight of the strikingly handsome man who had once been her lover and best friend standing a few feet away with his brother, Brett. She'd met Brett once when he'd come to visit Carson at college.

Her attention moved swiftly back to Carson, and she was unable to look away. His white dress shirt was rolled up to his elbows, revealing muscular forearms, and tucked into perfectly tailored dark slacks. He was broader now, tall, and sturdy. A big, beautiful man with the classic good looks of a 1950s movie star. He raked a hand through his short hair, laughing at something Brett must have said. His familiar laughter made her knees weak.

Please look over.

No. Don't. Her heart might explode.

Wait. Yes, look over.

Oh God.

What was she doing? She was a professional, educated woman. She should not be weak-kneed over the sight of a man. But apparently her body didn't get the memo, because her pulse skyrocketed, and she could barely breathe. She gripped the handle of her suitcase tighter, using it for balance. Carson turned, his chiseled features softened by the hint of a five-o'clock shadow. Their eyes connected, and his brows knitted, his jaw tensed.

Disappointment clutched her. Didn't he recognize her? Or *did* he? Was he angry? She should walk away, but she was pinned in place by his riveting gaze.

"HEY, ISN'T THAT your friend from college?" Brett, Carson's youngest brother and business partner, asked.

"Yeah," Carson answered, hearing the disbelief in his own voice. "I'll catch up with you another time." He couldn't take his eyes off Tawny Bishop, one of his closest friends from college, and the woman he'd compared all other women to ever since. *Tawny Klein*, he reminded himself. That went down like shattered glass. She'd gotten married right after college, and he'd been forced to let her go—*completely*.

Brett said something, but Carson was already on the move, eating up the distance between him and Tawny. Jesus, she looked *phenomenal*. Her gorgeous green eyes were locked on him, giving away her nervousness *and* her interest.

She's married, you asshole.

Maybe the interest he saw was wishful thinking. He'd spent long nights fantasizing about her entrancing eyes, her full, luscious lips, and, as strange as it sounded in his own head, her *mind*. People considered Carson a genius, and he knew Tawny was a level above, which was a huge turn-on. His fingers itched to touch her silky, strawberry-blond hair. She wore it shorter now, framing her beautiful face just above her shoulders. *Still long enough to tug?* He'd always loved her shoulders, though she'd usually kept them hidden, as they were now. But her pretty coat didn't hide her magnificent long legs, which disappeared beneath a sexy little black dress. Ten years was a long damn time, and here she was, standing before him like a gift. Maybe there was a Santa Claus after all.

"*Tabs.*" He reached for her, embracing her too hard and too long, but *damn*. She smelled feminine, and heavenly familiar even after all these years. *My Tabby*. The nickname had come without thought, and brought an unstoppable smile. She reminded him of a sweet, cuddly kitten. She'd always been more comfortable staying in than going out. She used to tutor kids Fridays and Saturdays, and she claimed to have too much studying to do afterward to go out, but he'd known she wasn't comfortable at parties or in crowds with strangers. They'd spent hours studying together Monday through Thursday, and those nights usually ended with Tawny cuddled up against his side in a purely platonic way, watching one sci-fi show or another and eating Junior Mints. But Sunday nights she'd been *his*. Truly his. At least that's how things were before the single most wonderful, and awful, night of his life.

"Carson."

Her warm breath whispered over his cheek. Desire spiked up his spine, as if no time had passed. She was finally here, in his arms—*and married*. He forced himself to release her, instantly missing the press of her lush curves against him. Her lips parted in the sweetest smile, the one that had first captured his attention.

Devastating.

Delicious.

Dangerous.

She was the only woman who had the power to unravel him with one look, one touch. He could run a marathon, bench three hundred and fifteen pounds, and take down the stealthiest hackers, but when it came to Tawny, he was powerless in so many ways.

"You look incredible." His gaze slid down her body, and she gripped the handle of her luggage tight, her knuckles blanching. Her eyes and that move sent conflicting messages of desire and fear. "What are you doing in the city?"

She blinked several times, as if she were weighing her answer. He desperately wanted to pull her into his arms again, but she wasn't his to touch. He pushed a hand into his pocket to keep from reaching for her.

Tawny tucked her hair behind her ear—a nervous habit he'd seen her do hundreds of times. She inhaled deeply and tilted her head a little, flashing another of his favorite smiles. The coy one that sent his mind down a dark path.

"I came to see you, actually," she finally answered.

"Me?" *Christ.* How long had he waited to hear those words? He stepped closer, his body thrumming with heat and hope. But goddamn, Carson didn't mess around with married women. Not even her. He forced himself to lean back on his heels, keeping a modicum of space between them.

"Yeah," she said with a whisper of a laugh. Another adorable nervous habit. "I heard about the fundraiser, and…" She shrugged. Her gaze skittered away for a beat, and when she looked at him again, the air around them ignited. "I miss you, Carson."

Aw, fuck. How was he supposed to resist her? "Tabs…? What's going on?"

She pressed her lips together, a flush rising on her cheeks, and she looked away again.

He respected her marriage. Her husband had been a good guy in college, even if a bit of a bore. But if he hurt her, all bets were off, and he'd have Carson to deal with. "Is everything all right with Keith?"

"Keith?" Her brow wrinkled in confusion. "Yes. Fine. We've been divorced for almost two years. But you probably know that, being one of the world's most renowned security experts. I'd imagine there's not much about me you *don't* know."

Carson uncovered things about people they thought they'd

buried forever. But after Tawny had gotten married, he'd allowed himself to delve into her personal life only once. Seeing her with her husband had been enough to keep him from ever doing it again. Now his emotions soared. If he'd known she'd gotten divorced, he would have been on her doorstep the next day.

"I'm sorry. I didn't know about your divorce." *But I'm glad I do now.* He took another step closer, noticing the darkening of her eyes. "I haven't looked you up since a short while after you were married."

"You…*Really?*" she asked softly.

"Yes."

"I never looked you up, either. Well, I poked around online once or twice, but that was a long time ago. I couldn't…" Her voice trailed off, and she quickly added, "I was just too busy."

Yeah, busy. You go with that, sweetheart. Go with whatever you need to feel better, because you're here now, and you're divorced, and I'm one hell of a lucky bastard. "Let's go someplace where we can talk."

"I need to find a hotel. This one is booked." She waved a piece of paper.

"Stay with me," came out before he could think, but he didn't regret it. The woman he'd loved for his entire adult life was finally within reach, and he wasn't about to let her go. This was his chance to figure out why he'd lost her, get to know her again, and make things right.

Uncertainty rose in her eyes.

"Come on, Tabs. You said you missed me. What better way to get reacquainted than hanging out like old times?" He slid a hand to the base of her neck, brushing his thumb over her cheek. Her breathing hitched, and he could see, and feel, it all right there beneath the veil of trepidation—passion and greed, vulnerability and sweetness.

"Carson," she whispered.

He'd heard that plea in his dreams so often, he was *this close* to lowering his lips to hers, reassuring her that he would keep her safe and make her happy. But just because she missed him didn't mean she was *ready* for him.

"I've got every episode of *X-Files* and *Firefly* and all your favorite sci-fi movies," he urged.

That sweet, sexy laugh slipped out again. He took her luggage from her hand and wrapped one hand around her waist, tugging her tight against him, making the decision for her. "Let's go, Tabs. You're staying with me. You can tell me all about how much you missed me."

"Carson…"

Selfishly soaking in the feel of her in his arms again, he said, "If you think I'm going to let you stay at a hotel, you're wrong. My place, Tabs. We just have to make one stop on the way."

"For what?"

"Junior Mints."

She laughed again, and his whole world seemed brighter. Damn, he'd missed her.

"Fine," she said. "But don't think I'm joining your harem. I came to see you, not sleep with you."

Ouch. Yeah, he'd had a harem back in college, but not by his doing. He'd never chased women. "How long are you in town?"

"Four days. Five nights."

He hauled her closer and gazed into her eyes. "I promise you, Tawny Bish—*Klein*—"

"*Bishop.* I went back to my maiden name."

That probably shouldn't make him feel good, but hell, she was Tawny Bishop once again. "I promise you, Tawny *Bishop*, I will not ask you to do anything you don't want to do."

"I know," she said a little breathlessly.

"I also promise you, when five nights pass, you won't want to get *out* of my bed."

She was quiet for a pensive second before saying, "Same old Carson."

"Not even close."

Chapter Two

TAWNY COULD COUNT on one hand the number of things in her life that had come easily. Anything academic was a given. She'd been blessed with genes from her MENSA-worthy father, who had been a chemist, and her mother, a biologist whom she'd lost before she was old enough to really know her. It was Tawny's academic prowess that had first connected her to Carson. They'd partnered for a lab, and she'd been sure he was a jocky, cocky twerp—until he'd opened his mouth and she'd learned that while he might have the hard body typical of athletes, he was beyond brilliant. As for cocky, well, he hadn't been in-your-face arrogant, but he could bring a woman to her knees with one heated glance, and that had been enough to set off her alarm bells. Her ability to discern bullshit from truth was another thing that had come easily from a very young age, which had immediately affected the third and final thing that had come without effort.

Her friendship with Carson.

He had immediately quelled those alarm bells with his careful, thoughtful nature, and their friendship had come as naturally as walking or talking. Carson's eye contact, his inquisitive nature, and his blatant answers, even when they could have used tempering, had instantly endeared her to him. She'd double majored in chemistry and computer science, giving them plenty to talk about. His love of science fiction had been icing on the cake. Now, as she sat beside him in the back of the dark sedan, shielded from his driver's view by tinted glass, his intoxicating scent incited seductive memories, spreading heat like wildfire through her body. His eyes never left hers. Except when the driver, whom Carson called Barton, stopped for Carson to purchase Junior Mints. He'd always been a man of his word.

She wasn't surprised he had a driver, with his career and his need for privacy. But the sparks still sizzling between them were surprising, even though some part of her had hoped—*assumed?*—their relationship would feel as right as it always had. Now another part of her was scared shitless. What if she couldn't handle it again?

Isn't that why I'm here? To figure this out?

When five nights pass, you won't want to get out of my bed.

She'd played off his comment as if it were an old joke between them, but they both knew he'd never said anything like that to her before. Not even close, which was why her heart was racing. He'd spoken with such confidence and finality. She thought she'd been prepared for anything, but she suddenly felt vulnerable, unable to decipher whether he meant what he said, or if this was one of his sexual games. His arm was stretched behind her, his fingers playing with the ends of her hair. While it was a familiar thing he'd done when they were younger, things had definitely changed. This was anything but easy. It was *combustible.*

She swallowed hard. *Maybe this is a little too much like old times.* Their connection was electric. *Visceral.* She definitely hadn't blown that out of proportion. *Am I setting myself up for more heartache?* Was this going to be just like college all over again—she'd fall for Carson while he played around with a host of other women?

He pushed his hand to the base of her neck, rubbing the knots that had been there since she'd first seen the flyer for the fundraiser. She closed her eyes, enjoying his touch. It had been years since she'd been touched by a man, and no one had ever touched her in the way, sexual or platonic, that Carson did. Trust had never been an issue between them. The foundation of trust they'd built helped push her worries away.

"That feels incredible."

"You always did carry your stress in your neck."

The seductive way he said it reminded her of how he'd soothed the lingering aches from her neck and shoulders after he'd bound her to the bed. She'd melted beneath his touch then, just as she was doing now.

"You remember?" She opened her eyes and found him watching her even more intently than before.

"I haven't forgotten a thing, Tabs." He ran his finger along the edge of her jaw. "Not one second of the time we spent together."

He leaned closer, and she fought against her body's natural inclination to meet him halfway. *Tell me you want my mouth.*

"Close your eyes, Tabs. Relax."

She closed her eyes, comforted by his taking control even though he hadn't asked for what she wanted. This was better. *Smarter.*

"Tell me about your divorce. Was it amicable? Or do I have to track down Keith and make him disappear?"

She smiled, eyes still closed, his hand working its magic on her tension. "It was friendly. We weren't in love, at least not the way married couples should be." *He was safe. But he wasn't you.*

"We're still friends."

"I'm sorry you weren't happy, but I'm glad it didn't end painfully."

He leaned closer, his breath warming her skin, drenching her in the scent of rum. *Dark rum.* Sweet and spicy, with hints of sugarcane, molasses, and charred oak. *Oh,* what she'd give to taste it on him, to feel the hard press of his lips, his tongue sliding over hers as he took the kiss deeper, until he possessed all of her. She opened her eyes, and he was *right there,* close enough to fulfill her every wish.

The car pulled to the side of the road, and the edges of Carson's lips tipped up, as if he knew exactly what she'd been thinking. She was sure he did, which made her even more nervous.

"I've missed you, too, Tabs," he said as Barton opened the car door and cold air rushed over her legs. "Let's get you inside."

Carson stepped out and helped her from the car, his hand resting on her back as he guided her under his umbrella, which seemed to appear out of nowhere.

Barton carried her bag to the porch and drove away as stealthily as a ninja. Carson tucked her against him as they hurried up the brick steps of his Gramercy Park home. Ornate iron railings and brick columns framed an inviting front porch. He set the umbrella against the brick wall and pushed a code into a keypad by the door. The sound of a lock unlatching competed with the thump of her rampant heartbeat. His hand moved lower, his long fingers pressing against the base of her spine as he pushed the door open.

His alluring scent wafted out of his home like an embrace. She noted the strength of his hand, and his commanding presence, as they stepped inside, and he set her bags in the high-ceilinged foyer. She inhaled deeply, taking in the expansive living room off to the right. Sleek-lined and tufted black leather sofas were complemented by a white marble coffee table. A stately and elegant fireplace was centered along the far wall, flanked by built-in bookshelves, and beside them, black-and-white artwork that looked like it cost a fortune. His style hadn't changed much. He'd always preferred clean, smooth lines, though his furniture in college hadn't been nearly as expensive. She wondered for the first time if her affinity for the same was born from their friendship or if she'd developed it before they'd met. She could barely remember her life before Carson, and she wondered if he was as nervous as she was. Some people emitted unpleasant odors when they were nervous, and others simply smelled a little *different*. Tawny had never been able to smell Carson's nerves. He was the most even-keeled, controlled person she knew.

Except when they'd roll the dice to see who got to take sexual control and he'd lost, handing the reins over to her. She'd gotten a taste of what it was like to *take* and *demand*, and he'd gotten a dose of vulnerability. She shuddered with the illicit memories.

"Cold?" Carson asked as he removed her coat and hung it in a closet behind him.

"A little." *But that's not why I shuddered.*

He pulled out his phone, scrolling and tapping, then slipped it back into his pocket. She heard the lock mechanisms in the door again, and a fire *whoosh*ed to life in the fireplace. His gaze moved hungrily down her body, leaving a trail of goose bumps in its wake. He pressed his large, rough hands to her upper arms, moving them from shoulder to elbow and back up again, warming and exciting her at once. When he reached her shoulders, he touched the leather accent on the capped sleeves of her dress.

"Leather. Nice touch." His eyes darkened.

"I thought you might like it." She'd picked out the dress with him in mind after she'd first gotten divorced, but it had taken her two years to get up the courage to come see him.

He squeezed her shoulders the way he used to when he'd strip her bare. How had she gone so many years without him? Without his touch? His voice? His intimate knowledge of her?

"I would like you in rags, Tabs."

She knew how true that was. She had never been the type of girl to wear cute little skirts and sandals or plunging necklines. That hadn't come until she was older, trying to entice her husband into sexier thoughts. A futile endeavor, and a painful one for her. It was no wonder she couldn't lure Keith into something more. He'd always known it was Carson she wanted.

"Well, that's about all I wore in college, so…"

"No one filled out jeans and T-shirts the way you did." His gaze took another stroll down her body. "And that dress…*man*, Tabs."

He led her across the hardwood floors as she soaked in his compliment, and the rest of the living room came into view. It was much more expansive than she'd thought, with another sofa, a leather recliner with a reading light beside it, which made her want to curl up with a good book, and floor-to-ceiling glass doors that opened to a balcony.

"Can I get you something to drink?" he asked.

That was a dangerous question, and she knew by the seductiveness of his voice that he was thinking the same thing. He was testing her boundaries, something he was *very* good at. The silent question—*Are we going there tonight?*—lingered in his eyes. She hadn't been a drinker in college, and the one and only time she had given in to his persistent suggestion of attending a party together, it had taken only one drink to lower her defenses enough for her to reach for his hand when the noisy crowd had made her nervous. The second drink had loosened her up enough to dance with him when he dragged her to the middle of the room and began moving in ways she'd seen only in movies. And the third drink, which they'd had in his apartment later that Sunday night, had been enough for her to surrender to her hidden desires—and then some.

In the years since, she'd honed her ability to have two or three drinks without losing control. A drink was exactly what she needed to fend off her nerves.

"Yes, please."

"MÉNAGE À TROIS?" Carson handed Tawny a glass and sank down on the couch beside her, enjoying the shock flaring in her eyes. He was pleased to find this boundary, as he'd wondered how far she'd taken her passions over the years. "Don't worry," he said gently, then firmer, "I'm not into sharing. It's the name of the drink."

Sighing with relief, she took the glass and held it under her nose, breathing it in. He'd always loved watching her take in the scent of everything from books to food. But his favorite thing was when they were close and she'd run her nose over his skin, breathing *him* in.

"Mm. Dark rum, triple sec, and cream?"

"Fascinating. You've still got that keen sense of smell."

She lifted the glass toward her lips, and as he'd remembered, her tongue swept across the rim just before she took a drink. He felt the warm glide as if it had slicked over his skin.

"It's what I do for a living," she said, and set her glass on the coffee table. Turning toward him, she curled her legs up on the couch. Her dress inched up her thighs, and he couldn't help but appreciate the view. "I'm a perfumer, in Paris."

She'd only just reappeared and his mind was already sprinting through a list of possible entanglements with her life being so far away. "A perfumer? You did it. When you took that internship with the fragrance company, you said you'd find your way to the top. And Paris? I guess that's where the magic happens for fragrances?"

"Yes, but that's not the only reason why I moved there." She tucked her hair behind her ear, her gaze falling to the space between them. "Paris was my escape to start over. I moved there about two years ago, after my father passed away."

She stretched her arm across the back of the couch and rested her cheek on it, her green eyes finding his once again. His heart sliced right down the middle at the pain in her eyes, the same way it had all those years ago, the night she'd ended their sexual relationship and run out of his apartment. Only this time he could try to ease the pain in a way he'd never been given a chance to back then.

He hooked his hand beneath her knees, lifting her legs over his as he moved closer. Her father had been her world. She'd called him every week all four years of college, and she'd sent him letters in the mail. *He and my mother used to send each other letters. I think it makes him happy to get mail other than bills.* And every year on her parents' anniversary, she and her father would have lunch together at the coffeehouse in Greenwich Village where her parents first met. He couldn't begin to imagine how alone she must feel.

She snuggled closer, placing her hand on his stomach and resting her cheek on his arm, underscoring how deep and easy their friendship had been. It was like time hadn't changed anything at all. But he knew it had. Time had given him a deeper understanding of who he was and what he wanted. And he'd come to understand that what he'd felt for Tawny all those years ago had been love, and even now, years later, that love was still alive.

He pressed a kiss to her forehead. "I'm so sorry. I wish I had been there for you."

"I do, too," she whispered sweetly, driving the ache deeper. "But you couldn't have been there without turning my world even more upside down than it already was. It was a really difficult time for me, and my father's death was just part of the reason. After he died I couldn't bring myself to go through his belongings. He'd pared down to the essentials before he got really sick. I had no idea he'd been so sick until I came home for the holidays and I noticed the house looked emptier. He told me then that the cancer wasn't getting better, and he said he didn't want me to have to weed through his life."

She paused, staring across the room as if she was remembering the moment he'd said it. "Anyway, I put his things into storage and sold the house. I still can't face going through them."

He brushed her hair from her cheek, wondering how many other things she'd experienced without someone by her side. "You shouldn't face that alone. I'll go with you. We'll take care of it tomorrow."

"You'd do that for me? I can't promise I won't fall apart. My dad had been sick for a long time. I should have been ready for the end, but it was awful."

"How can you ever be ready to lose someone you love? I'll be there with you, and if you fall apart, I'll put you back together." When his little sister had been diagnosed with leukemia, it had happened so fast, they'd had no time to prepare. It seemed like one day she was sick with a bad rash and then the next they were in the hospital. And then she was gone.

Her whole body seemed to sigh with relief. "Thank you," she said softly.

"Do you want to talk about your dad?"

She nodded, gratitude rising in her eyes. "I was with him in the days before he passed. He'd lost a huge amount of weight, Carson. It was hard to see his body withering away after he'd been my rock for so long. But really, he was my rock even then, frail or not. He was days from leaving this world forever, and I think he made a point of saving *me* by saying something that changed the way I looked at my life, and myself."

"I can only imagine how difficult that was. I'm here now, and you can count on me, Tabs. I'll help you with whatever you need. What did he say that made such a difference?"

She smiled, and that nervous laugh slipped out again. "Well, you knew my dad. You know how serious he was."

He'd met her father a few times, but one time stood out in his mind. He'd come to visit when Carson and Tawny had been cramming for a test. They'd had dinner together, and they'd spent the evening discussing family, science, and plans for their futures. It had been an unforgettable night, and not just because of their instant camaraderie, but because her father had reminded Carson of his own father before his sister had died from leukemia, when his father had turned bitter and angry.

"He *was* a serious guy, but that's what I liked about him,"

Carson said. "He was honest and real. And in this messed-up world where people have seventeen fake personas on social media and get off on naked Snapchat pics, we need more people like him."

"He was an acquired taste for some. Like I am." She smiled up at him.

"Acquired taste my ass." *I'd call you an obsession.* "Babe, you're the realest person I know." He lifted her hand from his stomach and brushed his thumb over the fingers that had once explored his body with such intense curiosity it brought a dull ache. "The world is full of ignorant people who can't understand complexities. They're limited, and not always because of cognitive abilities, but because they have no drive to expand their views, which allows them only to fit people into their narrow idea of *typical*. Those dullards are a dime a dozen. They're shallow, and unambitious, and they couldn't pick out a diamond among a heap of rocks."

He pressed a kiss to the back of her hand and gazed into her eyes. "You are not an *acquired* taste, Tawny. You're the piece of computer code only the most adept can read. Fine silk in a sea of polyester. Godiva in a bucket of Hershey's."

She laughed and buried her face in the crook of his arm. "Carson, I've missed our friendship so much." She looked up at him again, a sweet smile playing on her lips. "Do you really want to know what he said?"

"What do you think?"

"I think you only say what you mean." Her expression grew serious. "I asked him if he had any regrets, and he said, 'How can I have any regrets? I spent every minute I could with the love of my life.' He meant my mother, of course."

"Yeah, I got that."

"Then he said, 'And she left me with the greatest gift of all.'"

He brushed his lips over her forehead. "That's you, Tabs."

"Yeah, I got that," she said with a sassy arch of her brow. "He was on oxygen, and he paused for the longest time. I thought that was all he had to say. I don't mean like it was *only* that, because I felt like what he'd said was significant. But a few minutes later he asked me to get a mirror, and when I did, he told me to look in it. Then he asked if I had any regrets. I couldn't answer him, Carson. If I was looking at him, I know I would have said *no* just so he wouldn't worry about me when he took his last breath. But looking in that mirror? He forced me to see who I'd become, like he knew how unhappy I was. He said, 'Regret comes from living your life wearing someone else's skin. It's fixable.'"

She shrugged, but he could see the shrug was an act to cover up how affected she'd been.

"After he passed away, I vowed to figure out my life. I separated from Keith and took a job in Paris with a fragrance company that had been trying to recruit me forever. I decided to stop living an unfulfilling life, and I spent the last couple of years trying to figure out what that meant, and who I was."

"You're killing me here," he admitted. "All this time I thought you were happily married. What happened, Tawny?"

"You, Carson. You happened."

Chapter Three

THE GENTLE SOFTNESS in Tawny's voice captivated Carson, but he didn't know how to interpret her comment. Was she blaming him for the demise of her relationship? He'd avoided her at all costs to keep that from happening. As badly as he wanted her to be *his*, he would never want to be the cause of the failure of her marriage.

"Tabs, I'm not sure I understand. I haven't seen you since graduation."

He was still holding her hand, absently brushing his thumb over her fingers, watching as she contemplated her response. The pulse in the base of her neck quickened, and she swallowed hard again. She lifted her beautiful eyes to his, tides of emotion welling within them as she turned her hand over, revealing her palm.

His chest swelled with the simple motion.

When he was younger, he'd thought his love of rough sex and his penchant for silk ties and sexual exploration had set him apart from others in a negative way. His friends were having typical college-age hookups: missionary, doggy style, and blow jobs. While those aspects were enjoyable, Carson had craved more from the time testosterone had let loose in his teenage body. He'd tried to play out his fantasies with a few different girls, but they'd been turned off by a tug of their hair or the command in his voice—commands he was unable, or unwilling, to temper in the heat of the moment. He'd learned to keep that side of himself locked away, zoning out during sex, using it solely as a means to find release. Then he'd met Tawny. They'd been paired off for a chemistry lab, and their connection was immediate. Not just because Tawny was hot as sin, but she was smart, kept her nose to the grindstone, and above all, she respected herself. Carson craved respect, and not just for himself. If a woman didn't respect herself, then how could he? For that reason alone, he hadn't had many sexual partners—at least not as many as people seemed to think.

With Tawny things had moved swiftly from the lab to friendship, and they'd claimed Monday through Thursday evenings as *theirs*. It had happened seamlessly, and before long, they counted on each other for more than just help with academics. Whatever Tawny needed—a willing ear to vent to, a friend to have lunch with, someone by her side when she was sick—Carson was there for her, and vice versa. *Outside* the bedroom. That was a line they hadn't talked about but had somehow understood existed. Carson had been attracted to Tawny from day one, and two years into their friendship, he couldn't take it any longer, and he'd pushed her out of her comfort zone. That night changed everything.

One party.

A few drinks.

A single kiss and the line was crossed. A second kiss had almost completely erased the line. Tawny had known of his desire to remain single, though she'd never known his reasons. She'd respected his need for privacy and freedom. At first she didn't seem to have issues with it, and allowing his true self to come out in the bedroom with her wasn't a question. He couldn't have resisted those urges if he'd tried, which surprisingly, he hadn't. He'd never known why that was, but through their almost two years of Sunday-night sexual exploration, he'd come to understand himself better. He wasn't a dominant, and he wasn't a deviant. He didn't have a dire need to control in order to get off, and he didn't demand submissiveness in his partner. He didn't have a name for what he was, because he had only allowed himself to be that man with Tawny. She'd brought it out in him, encouraging and accepting him without question. What they had didn't need defining. They'd fallen into sharing secret, wordless signals regarding their moods and desires. And then there were the dice. *Man*, he loved the dice.

She was giving him a signal now, turning her palm up. She was *his*, at least for tonight, and as heat rushed like rivers through his veins and he lifted her hand to his lips, trepidation stepped in. She'd broken him when she'd ended their sexual relationship and started dating, then married, Keith, and he'd respected her too much to try to change her mind. He was older, wiser, but was he emotionally stronger?

He placed her hand flat on his chest, silently telling her to leave it there as he caressed her thigh. "Tell me I didn't kill your marriage."

"You didn't," she said a little shakily. "Memories of us did."

Memories of them had ruined her marriage? The same way they'd ruined him for any other woman? He had so many questions, but she licked her lips, leaving them slick and enticing, unmistakable passion burning in her eyes, and his need for answers got lost in a surge of desire. She knew how much he loved her lips. He'd told her often enough, though only on Sunday nights. That part of their life had been kept separate from the rest, but she was giving him the green light now. She was here for five nights, and he'd gone without her for too long. He wasn't about to turn down her invitation.

Her eyes darkened as he pushed his hand along her smooth, soft thigh and beneath her dress, feeling the rough brush of lace at the top of her thigh-high stockings, the soft expanse of her bare ass, and the sliver of a thong across her hip. He brushed his lips over hers, tracing her lower lip with his tongue. Her breath left her lungs in a needy sigh, and her fingers dug into his chest.

"I never meant to hurt you." His hand splayed over her thigh, inching toward the heat radiating from her center.

"I know," she said hungrily.

He pushed his other hand into her hair, threading his fingers in the silky strands and taking hold—unraveling a decade of knots inside him. Lightning flared in her eyes, and it reached deep into his core, calling to the parts of himself he'd repressed for so long and lifting them out of the darkness.

"I've missed your face, Tawny. Your voice, your *touch*," he confessed.

He lowered his lips to hers, taking his first taste of her and reveling in her sweet familiarity. His insides burst to life as he plundered her glorious mouth. His hand fisted tighter, tugging her head to the angle he craved as he intensified the kiss. She was his safe haven, his perfect match, and she was kissing him with all of herself, making those sinful noises that had fueled his fantasies and had always driven him mad. He thrust his hand between her legs, stroking her through her sexy-as-fuck lace thong as he lowered her to the couch.

"God, Tabs, your mouth. I've missed your fucking mouth."

He reclaimed her lips, more demanding this time, relishing the slickness it spurred between her legs. It had been so long, he felt like a starving man eating for the first time, and somehow he also felt like no time had passed. Her kisses, her scent, and the feel of her hand clutching his skin like she never wanted to let him go were exhilarating. He teased and stroked until her panties were drenched and she was writhing, whimpering into his mouth. Her body was more than a wonderland; it was a *world* in and of itself, responsive and desirous, impossible to deny. He pushed her panties aside as he drew back from the kiss and dragged his fingers lightly over her slick heat. She was shaved bare, just the way he loved her.

"Open your eyes," he demanded. "I want to see what I'm doing to you."

He brushed his thumb over her clit as she opened her eyes, and she sucked in a sharp breath. She needed this as much as he did. His fingers played over her wet flesh, teasing and taunting, and when her hips rose, urging him to take more, he withdrew from between her legs. She whimpered, and he brought his glistening fingers to his lips and slicked his tongue over them, tasting her sweetness. A guttural moan tore from his lungs, like she was the sustenance he needed to survive. He rubbed those fingers over her lips and pushed them gently into her mouth. Christ, she was incredibly sexy as her tongue moved over his fingers without question. It had been too long.

"Suck."

She held his gaze, her lips closing around his fingers. She was so beautiful and trusting, he wanted to strip her bare and take his fill, but he was in no rush to get hurt again. He needed to understand what had happened all those years ago and why she was really there. He kissed her again, tasting her arousal, drawn deeper into her with every breath. He pushed his hand between her legs again, squeezing her thigh and teasing her with his thumb, earning a greedy moan.

"Touch me," he said.

Her soft, delicate hand moved to his cheek, cupping his jaw, sliding over his neck, and up into his hair. While other women would go straight for his cock, Tawny knew just how to touch him, and the tension drained from his body. She dragged her nails down the back of his neck, a seductive grin lifting her lips as she dug them into his skin just below his collar. He fucking loved that. He unbuttoned his shirt and stripped it off, drinking in her ravenous gaze as it traveled over his chest and down his abs. He set his shirt aside as she rose beneath him, her soft hands and sweet lips trailing over his pecs. She sealed her mouth over his nipple, clamping down hard.

"*Fuck*, baby, you feel good."

Her gaze flicked up, watching him as she dragged her tongue over the bite marks. He fisted his hand in her hair, holding her tight against him as she sucked and licked and drove him out of his mind. He yanked her head back and crushed his mouth to hers, wanting everything and knowing he needed to slow down and make sure her head—*and her heart*—were in the same place before he put his whole self on the line. But slowing down was not something he could do when everything he craved was right there in his arms.

He pushed to his feet, bringing her up beside him. She tucked her hair behind her ear and lowered her trembling hand to her side. She was so real, nervous and eager at once. He moved behind her and unzipped her dress, leaving it open as he stepped in front of her, searching her eyes for hesitation. Raw, unbridled passion stared back at him. He gently lifted her dress off her shoulders and let it tumble around her feet, exposing her gorgeous figure. Her ivory breasts strained behind black lace. The thin strips of her thong rode high on her full hips. Her thigh-high stockings looked even darker against her creamy skin.

"You are flawless and feminine." He ran his fingers up her ribs, and she shivered. "Feel what you do to me."

She palmed his throbbing cock through his slacks, and her lips parted.

"Stroke me."

She obeyed, holding his gaze. Her touch was perfect, tight and firm. It took all of his control not to strip his pants off and push her to her knees. She was biting her lower lip, her signal that she wanted him to do just that. Her cues were as familiar as if no time had passed.

He ran his finger over her lips. "Tell me what you want."

"I want you in my mouth."

"Just hearing you say that makes me want to fuck your mouth, but I won't." He cupped her cheek, brushing his thumb over her lower lip, and she sucked it into her mouth, swirling her tongue around it. Lust seared directly to his cock. He withdrew his thumb slowly, watching her tongue follow it out, licking all the way to the tip.

"Please," she begged. "I want to taste you."

"You know better than to try to rush me."

She pressed her lips together, a smile tugging at their edges.

He ran his hands down her arms. Her skin was hot from the fire. "I want to do everything at once. Drop to my knees and pleasure you." He kissed the swell of her breasts, and dragged his tongue along the deep crevice between them. "I want to bend you over the back of the couch and fuck you until you forget what it was like to have any other man inside you."

"Carson—" rushed from her lips.

He traced the edge of her stockings with his finger, and she held her breath.

"I want to lay you down and make love to every inch of your body, slowly and meticulously, until you are completely and totally *mine*." But anticipation was everything, and for now he filled his palms with her sweet ass and kissed her breasts through the lace. He sucked each taut peak, earning a string of seductive, needful sounds. His hands slid along the length of her thong, between the supple globes of her ass, and teased over her tightest hole.

"Carson, *please*—"

He took her in a punishingly intense kiss. A kiss to erase the questions in his mind about other men she'd been with since her husband. He intensified the kiss as he slid his fingers forward, soaking them with her arousal. He returned to the place that made her body tremble, teasing over her puckered flesh. She pressed her hips back against his hand, and he withdrew from between her legs.

He pushed his other hand into her hair and grabbed hold. "Are you *mine* for these five nights?" he asked roughly, wanting so much more.

"Yes," she said pleadingly.

"No running away."

"No," she said breathlessly. "I promise."

His love for her was all-consuming, urging him to give her everything she wanted. But he fought against it. There were lines he'd wait to cross until he was sure she was really his. She watched him intently as he took her hands and kissed each wrist the way he used to do before he bound them. He held both of her hands in one of his and reached for his dress shirt.

TAWNY'S BODY WAS on fire, her erratic heartbeat evident in the fast rise and fall of her breasts, as she watched Carson reaching for his dress shirt. He had been fit in college, but that was nothing compared to the strong man standing before her. Broad shoulders tapered in a heavily muscled V to the waist of his slacks. His shoulders and biceps flexed deliciously as he shook out his shirt and turned to face her. His handsome face was a mask of control, but even his serious dark eyes couldn't hide his primal hunger.

She drew in a deep breath, anticipating his shirt being wound around her wrists. She'd been frightened by the intensity of her desires when they were in college, when the mere touch of silk, the graze of his teeth on her flesh, would bring her to the verge of orgasm. Her need for their Sunday-night rendezvous had become an obsession, consuming her every thought. Just thinking about what they did together had made her wet and needy. She'd found herself fantasizing instead of paying attention in class, and when she and Carson had studied together toward the end of their time as lovers, she could barely hold herself together. She couldn't afford to be sidetracked, having secured a full academic scholarship, and that lack of control and fractured focus had frightened her. She'd thought she'd done the right thing by ending that part of their relationship, but even after, when they'd continued as friends, the heat never went away. She'd thought when she married Keith and moved to Chicago, cutting ties with Carson, her desires would eventually lessen, but they'd only grown stronger. And now she was practically salivating at the thought of Carson wrapping his dress shirt around her wrists, as he'd done so many times before.

She pressed her hands together and lifted them. *Take me, Carson. Please, take me.*

He inhaled an almost indiscernible breath, the one that let her know he'd made some kind of decision. It was a sigh she'd noticed the first night they'd studied together, one she couldn't miss. She didn't think he even realized he made it, though it preceded most of his bigger decisions. He reached behind her and draped his shirt around her shoulders, holding her steady as he bent to pick up her dress. She lifted each foot to free the material, confused by this turn of events.

He settled a hand on her lower back. "It's late, and we both need time to process this."

"But…?" She grasped for words. "Carson, I want this. I want you. That's why I'm here. To see…"

He gazed into her eyes, hurt lingering beneath his perfectly honed mask of control, which kept others at bay. That fateful night came rushing back. The incessant knocking at the door that had come when she'd been blindfolded and bound to his bedposts. She'd heard Carson send the woman away, but being caught in such a vulnerable position had stopped her cold. She'd known about his other trysts, and she'd somehow put them in a place in her mind where she could deal with them. Denial was a magnificent thing. But that nameless, faceless woman hadn't been the reason Tawny had ended things. It was the control those nights had over the rest of her life. That momentary interruption had simply given her an out, an excuse—and she'd taken it. Blaming his string of women and inability to commit—something she'd never asked him to do— had been an excuse he could understand. She knew he'd respected her enough to accept the renewed delineation in their friendship, and when she'd asked that they go back to being only friends, he'd agreed. That was when she'd found Keith. *Safe, reliable, vanilla Keith.*

She'd regretted ending her affair with Carson since the very second the words had left her lips, but she never imagined she'd hurt *him*.

Now he silently guided her toward the stairs, his way of telling her he wasn't ready to talk about it yet. She should respect his need for time and maybe even be thankful for the space to come to grips with, and try to understand, how quickly her desires had consumed her. But the first of her five nights was slipping through her fingers, and every hour without him would feel like a lifetime. She needed more in order to gain perspective on their relationship, or she'd be caught in this web of desire forever.

"Carson, I know this is out of the blue, but can we talk about it?" she asked as they ascended the stairs.

"Absolutely." He led her into a beautiful bedroom.

He turned her in his arms, the muscles in his neck and face corded tight. She knew that look of sexual repression. Hell, she'd mastered it.

"Tomorrow," he said evenly.

Carson wasn't exactly stubborn, but once he made up his mind about something, only *reason* would convince him otherwise. The trouble was, she had no rational reason for needing to have the conversation tonight, beyond her own selfish need for a resolution to her feelings. She rested her head on his chest, listening to the fast, steady beat of his heart.

"I'm sorry for showing up unannounced," she said softly.

He tipped her chin up, smiling down at her and healing the fissure that was quickly tearing at her insides.

"I'm not at all sorry that you showed up—announced or unannounced. I just..." He clenched his jaw. "I'll bring your things up. There are clean towels in the linen closet in the bathroom if you want to take a hot bath and relax."

"Thank you." *You remembered.* Of course he remembered. Beyond the hurt and desire, she saw the man she'd fallen in love with so long ago. *Caring, thoughtful, never-miss-a-thing Carson.* Not that they'd spent many nights sleeping over at each other's places, but Carson had always pampered her. After they made love, he'd draw a warm bubble bath and climb in with her, carefully washing her, rubbing the soreness from her muscles, making her feel wanted and loved. She'd missed that, too. She'd thought all men would be that thoughtful, but she'd quickly learned that wasn't the case.

"My bedroom's right down the hall."

Her heart sank. She understood not wanting to take things further tonight, but she'd thought she'd at least be in his arms. "This isn't your bedroom?"

He shook his head and held her face between his hands. "Tawny, you're here. I'm *not* sending you away or disregarding you. I shouldn't have taken things as far as I did downstairs, but…" He paused, brows knitted. "I want you here, but I can't take you into my bed until I understand the whole story." He kissed her softly. "Sleep well."

She watched him disappear down the hall, and for a moment she was thrown back in time to the party that had changed everything. Girls had been all over him from the minute he'd walked in. She'd gone to a few parties in college with her other friends, but they were more like gatherings to watch a movie or have pizza. They certainly were not the caliber of the party she'd attended with Carson, where kids were practically having sex out in the open. She remembered how nervous those other girls had made her, and the way Carson had tucked her safely beneath his arm. He'd never left her side, had included her in every conversation, and when he'd hauled her against him, dancing seductively, much of that nervousness had subsided. Being in his arms that night had been the start of a never-ending love affair. But was it *real?* Or were her emotions getting the better of her again?

She took a long hot bath, trying to clear her mind. As she dried off, she remembered how he used to help her from the tub, carefully drying her before tending to himself. She heard his shower running on the other side of the wall and pictured his hard body beneath the warm spray. Had he taken things into his own hands to ease his needs?

As she dried off, the sound of his shower silenced. She stared at the wall, wishing she were in the steamy bathroom with him. She was supposed to be figuring things out, not falling into bed with him.

She found her suitcase and purse on the bed. A note from Carson lay on top of one of his neatly folded T-shirts. Her heart pumped a little harder knowing he remembered how she used to love wearing his shirts. She read his neatly scripted note.

I'm glad you're here.

Simple. Direct. *Carson.*

My Carson.

She pressed his soft shirt to her face, inhaling deeply. He must have carried it against his chest, because it smelled like him. She slipped it over her head, put on a clean pair of panties, and sat on the edge of the bed, thinking about what he'd said. *I want you here, but I can't take you into my bed until I understand the whole story.*

She didn't know the whole story. How could she? She'd had no idea what to expect when she'd come to see him. She'd gone ten years craving *him*, not just a different type of sexual relationship. He'd been a permanent fixture in her life, even though he wasn't physically present. He was the invisible man in her bedroom, the voice whispering in her ear as she chose lingerie, towels, and bedsheets. Even in college, Carson had been particular about having soft, smooth textures against his skin.

Most of the time, she mused.

She ran her hand over the luxurious bedspread, trying to keep from wondering how many women had been in that bed.

In *his* bed.

She didn't even know if he was in another relationship. Her stomach clenched at that.

Yes, I do. I do know.

He never would have said, *When five nights pass, you won't want to get out of my bed*, if he hadn't meant it. And when she paired that with his comment about needing to understand the whole story, she saw him even more clearly. He was protecting himself from being hurt again. She wrapped her arms around her middle, feeling sick over having hurt him in the first place.

The control their sexual relationship had held over her hadn't dwindled one bit. It had gotten stronger, hotter, even more compelling than before. But *she'd* gotten stronger, too. She'd set out to gain perspective, but now all she needed was Carson.

Her phone vibrated, and she dug it out of her bag. Keith's name flashed on the screen, and she sighed. Carson hadn't been the only thing that had driven a wedge between her and Keith. From the time Tawny was a teenager, she'd volunteered tutoring children who were in the foster care system, and she'd continued during college. While other kids had spent their weekends partying, she'd spent her time acting like an older sister to little boys and girls. After she and Keith had married, she'd wanted to begin fostering children, but Keith hadn't been interested. He'd thought they would be taking on someone else's problems. Wasn't that the point? Those *someone elses* had left behind children who needed love. When she'd moved to Paris, she'd begun volunteering at an orphanage, and she'd done more than tutor. She'd fallen in love with a little girl named Adeline. Over the course of two years, they'd gotten tremendously close. Tawny had been teaching her English since they first met, and Adeline had soaked it up like a sponge. Without Keith to hold her back, Tawny had even allowed herself to think about fostering Adeline, but she worked too many hours to care for her properly.

Her phone rang again with a call from Keith. She answered, and before she could say hello, Keith said, "Hey. I was worried."

If she was ever going to figure out her life and move forward, it was time to define very clear boundaries with Keith.

"I'm sorry, and I'm fine. Keith, I appreciate your concern, but we've talked about my needing space to move on, and I think you need to focus your energies elsewhere."

"Tawny, when you get hurt, you're going to need my support."

She'd never told him anything about her and Carson's relationship other than the fact that they were good friends who had studied together. She'd never even admitted to sleeping with him. That was too private a detail to share, but she knew he'd surmised as much. When she and Keith had divorced, he'd told her that he'd known she was always in love with Carson and she hadn't denied it. She might have spent a decade confused, but she wasn't a liar.

"I know you think I will," Tawny said. "But I'm a big girl,

Keith. I can pick myself up and carry on. I've done it before. I'm sorry for not being the woman you needed, and I take that blame with a great amount of regret. You deserved more from a wife. But now it's time for me to be the woman *I* need to be. And I can't do that while I'm still tethered to you."

They talked for a few minutes, and though Keith tried to convince her otherwise, when they hung up, Tawny felt like she'd finally been unleashed from another part of her past that had been holding her back.

She pushed to her feet and peered out of the bedroom. The house was quiet as she walked down the hall and stood outside Carson's bedroom door, needing to be in his arms. She wanted to apologize and say all the things she should have told him back in college. She heard him pacing, and her stomach tumbled. What if while he was *processing*, he decided he didn't want to go where they'd already gone? What if he thought it was a mistake to invite her home with him?

She turned away from the door, her arms crossed over her churning stomach.

I didn't come all this way to chicken out.

Drawing in a deep breath—she was living on deep breaths lately—she reminded herself that the only way to get through this was to face it head-on. Fear tiptoed in again with the possibility of this intrusion going wrong. She drew her shoulders back, knowing she should *not* need a man to feel whole. She had enough money to buy anything she'd ever need. She had a unique skill set that separated her from others, and a solid job, even if it wasn't the one she truly wanted. She should walk right back to her bedroom and deal with it in the morning, when she wasn't tired and all revved up. But right then what she *should* do, and *reality*, were a world apart. She'd been a fool to think she could move on from what they had together. Carson owned a piece of her, and how could she ever feel complete again without reclaiming it?

Without him?

His door swung open, and he barreled out, stumbling into her.

"Tabs?" he said with as much shock as relief. He grabbed her around the waist to keep her from toppling over. His hair was damp, and he was naked, save for a pair of tight black briefs that left nothing to her imagination.

"Sorry, I…" *Just needed to be in your arms.*

He exhaled a long breath. Hurt and desire brewed in his expression.

She bit her lower lip to keep anxious tears at bay. Then his arms were around her, one hand pressed to her lower back, the other cradling the base of her skull, holding her safe and warm against his chest. He smelled so good, felt so right. How could she ever have walked away from him?

"It's okay," he said in a gravelly voice. "I've got you."

I've got you. He'd used those three words every time they'd tried something new in the bedroom, and come to think of it, every time he noticed she was having a hard time with pretty much anything. He'd always taken care of her, and the words alone calmed her, but combined with his embrace, she felt like she'd come home.

He led her into his bedroom and pulled back the comforter, telling her more than words ever could. She climbed between the lavish sheets and he settled in behind her, his hips cradling hers as he pulled the blanket over them and wrapped his arms around her. She crossed her arms over his, the fatigue of her trip catching up to her. She felt like an open wound being dressed for the first time, and she melted against him, safe and warm. *This* was exactly what she needed.

He was exactly what she needed.

"Carson?"

"Hm?"

"I never meant to hurt you, either."

He exhaled long and slow, as if he'd been waiting to hear that for a very long time. "I know, Tabs. I know."

Chapter Four

CARSON HAD HOPED that having Tawny in his arms again would be enough to satiate his appetite. But when he'd woken up at five o'clock, their bodies twined together like Twizzlers, he'd been hard as steel, and the urge to *have* her was overwhelming. She was exhausted and had fallen asleep almost instantly in his arms. Jet lag was a bitch. He slipped from the bed and paced, debating the obvious. Be a dick, wake her, and take his fill before they had a chance to talk, or get the hell out of there and let her rest. He could still taste her sweet kisses from last night.

She made a contented sound in her sleep, jarring him from his thoughts. He adored her too much to wake her.

A five-mile run in the cold November air helped clear his head. He went up to shower and found her looking heavenly, still fast asleep in his bed. She'd moved to his side, hugging his pillow. Why did that make him smile? Her pretty strawberry-blond hair fanned out around her face. She looked as innocent and as beautiful as a porcelain doll. He stripped off his running shirt and tossed it in the hamper, skipped his shower so as not to wake her, and headed downstairs, thinking about the first time they'd landed in bed together. She'd been naive, having had only one lover before him. Every touch had been tentative, every kiss slow and careful, but it hadn't taken long for her to give in to the passion he'd felt humming beneath her skin. Their friendship had created a bond of trust that had pulled them both into a deeper realm.

He cooked bacon and eggs and popped a few pieces of bread into the toaster. He'd just finished setting breakfast on the table when she padded downstairs, smiling sleepily, his T-shirt dwarfing her figure. His eyes trailed down her body to the taut peeks poking out against her—*his*—shirt. She curled her toes under one foot, turning as she trapped her lower lip between her teeth, ogling his bare chest. He knew they should talk, but rational thinking took a backseat to desire, and he opened his arms. She came to him willingly, just as she had last night when he'd plowed into her in the hallway after futilely trying to forget she was just down the hall. Whether she was there temporarily, or looking for more, he'd wanted her *in his bed*.

"Mm," she said against his chest. "I got worried when I woke up alone. Then I smelled bacon and all thoughts of *you* went out the window."

"Damn bacon wins out every time." He cradled her face and touched his lips to hers, smiling at her playfulness. "If I had stayed in bed, no part of you would have been safe. I would have taken you every which way I could."

He tried to resist, but he was no match for how she affected him. He kissed her neck, breathing in the scent of Tawny Bishop in the morning. His new favorite smell. And he didn't stop, couldn't stop, there. He continued kissing and nipping her warm skin. She pressed her hands to his chest, teasing her fingers over his pecs, instantly arousing him. Her tongue swept over his nipple, and he closed his eyes, reveling in the feel of her as she played his body like a fiddle.

"Why would that have been bad?" she asked in a breathy

voice.

"I'm trying to remember the answer to that myself." He pulled her forward, his hands sliding over silk panties at the same moment she sucked his nipple *hard*. "*Fuck*, Tabs. Silk…?"

He grabbed her hair and yanked her mouth away from his chest, taking her in a deep, penetrating kiss. Her mouth was *made* for kissing, hot, welcoming, and so damn forgiving. Carson's control frayed with every stroke of her tongue.

"We need to talk," he said between kisses.

"I know," she panted out, going up on her toes and rubbing against him like a cat.

"Tabs—"

He kissed her deeply, probing her mouth as he wanted to probe her body. She made those sexy noises she'd made last night, and he lost it. He pushed his hand beneath her panties, dipping into her slick heat, and groaned. He still held her hair, keeping her titillating mouth on his as he pushed in deeper, seeking the spot that would make her cry out his name. She moaned into the kiss and thrust her hand into his running pants, fisting his cock. *Fuuuck*. Sounds of passion—hers and his—twined together into a chorus of desire.

"Are you on birth control?" he said. "Please tell me you're protected."

"Yes."

He crashed his mouth to hers, tearing off her panties as she tugged down his pants. He kicked them away and lifted her into his arms. Her fingers dug into his shoulders as her tight heat swallowed every inch of his shaft. They both stilled, fire burning in her eyes.

You're mine, Tabs. You'll always be mine, was on the tip of his tongue, but he couldn't say the words. Something in his gaze must have given his emotions away, because the fire in her eyes turned to something much deeper he was afraid to name.

"Give me your mouth," he growled.

Her lips came down hungrily over his, and the sounds of their urgent lovemaking echoed in the kitchen. She used his shoulders for leverage as he pumped his hips, holding her waist, helping her meet his demands. He stepped toward the table, clearing it with one sweep of his arm, sending dishes and breakfast crashing to the floor. Tawny laughed into their kiss, making him laugh, too. *God, that laugh.* He set her on the edge of the table and took one of her legs in each hand, holding them on either side of his chest as he pounded into her. She leaned back on her palms, allowing him to take her harder, deeper. With one hand, she reached behind his neck and pulled him into a kiss. She was still so flexible it blew his mind.

"Harder," she pleaded against his mouth.

That's my girl. He released her legs, and she wound them around his waist. He grabbed her hips, holding her so hard he'd probably leave bruises as he slammed into her, wanting to brand her from the inside out, to feel all the heat he'd missed for too long. He sped up his efforts until she was crying out with each thrust.

"Tighter," he commanded, and felt her thighs and sex clench. He brought one hand between her legs, knowing just how to take her over the edge.

"Oh God, *Carson*—"

"Mouth," he said, his hands too occupied to grab her head and pull her forward.

Her mouth captured his, and her hands clawed up his neck, into his hair, digging into his skin. He tugged her tighter against him, her thighs squeezing his waist as he quickened his pace.

She cried out, and he swallowed her pleas as her body quaked, pulsing hot and tight around his cock, taking him higher and higher, until pure, explosive pleasure tore through him. She rose off the table when she was midorgasm. Her arms circled his neck, her sex squeezing mind-blowingly tighter, and when her magnificent mouth claimed his, she took his orgasm from perfect to *exquisite*. The room spun, and their bodies were slick with sweat, as they kissed and bucked to the clouds and back.

"Christ, babe," he panted out.

He stumbled away from the broken dishes and sank down to the floor, holding her in his lap and trying to wrap his head around the emotions surging through him. He kissed her cheeks, her forehead, ran his fingers through her hair, massaging her scalp. He rubbed her hips with both hands. She was flexible, but damn, that angle had to hurt. She nuzzled against his neck, her body limp and sated, sweet mewing sounds of gratification filling his ears.

"Carson," she whispered.

When she said his name like that, full of passion, it made his heart beat a little stronger. "Yeah?"

"I miss this kind of *talking* with you."

He lifted her chin, drowning in the pool of emotion in her eyes, both of them smiling.

"I miss *being inside you*, too. *Talking, fucking, loving, laughing*." He lowered his mouth to hers, kissing her adoringly, the way he couldn't resist kissing her all those years ago—and then he took that kiss deeper, kissing her the way he needed to now, with too much love for her to miss.

When their lips parted, she placed her finger over his. "Wow," she whispered. "Your kisses." Her eyes swept over the broken dishes and scattered food on the floor. "So much for self-control." She stretched as far as she could, snagged a piece of bacon that was teetering on the edge of a napkin, and arched a brow.

"Sustenance," he said. "You're going to need your energy for later."

"A promise I'm looking forward to you keeping."

She stuck one end of the bacon in his mouth, taking the other end in hers, both of them laughing as they ate their way to a delicious bacon kiss that went on and on.

"I need to shower," she said sweetly.

"Is that an invitation?"

She traced his collarbone with her fingers. "Are you still willing to go with me today to go through my dad's stuff?"

"I never back down on my word, especially to you."

"Then *no*, it's not an invitation."

He bit her shoulder, earning a sharp gasp as she climbed from his lap and pulled him to his feet.

"No?" he challenged.

"Look at us." Her smile lit up her eyes. "You're buck naked, I've got *you* dripping out of me, and the kitchen looks like you've been ransacked, when really we're just sex maniacs—"

He hauled her against him and nibbled on her neck. "Your point?"

"*Lord*, I love that," she said breathlessly. "Wait. Stop." She pushed at him, wiggling out of his arms. "We have *zero* self-control. If we shower together, we're going to end up getting down and dirty, and then we won't go to the storage unit. We won't leave your house for the whole time I'm here, and now that I'm thinking about my dad's stuff again, I kind of want to get it over with."

He turned her by the shoulders and smacked her ass. "Get

out of here and shower before I decide to show you what you can do with your rational thinking."

She glanced over her shoulder with a challenge in her eyes. "Like *that's* going to make me want to leave this room any faster?"

He took a step toward her, loving when she taunted him. She squealed, and ran for the stairs looking so fucking cute he could barely stand it. Stifling his laughter, he followed her to the bottom of the steps and hollered up after her, "Don't make innuendos you don't intend to keep."

She hung over the railing on the landing above, smiling down at him. "Did you want to *talk* some more?" With a sultry look, she stripped off his shirt and tossed it down the stairs before sauntering off, naked, toward her room.

TAWNY WAS EDGY when they arrived at the storage building. She wished she'd taken Carson up on the joint shower to keep her mind off the task they were there to accomplish. Her mind swam with worries about what she might find among her father's things and how she'd feel when she saw them. There were so many storage units. What did people store there? Things that weren't worthy of remaining in their basements or attics? Or was the majority of the building filled with mementos of people who had passed away?

She reached for Carson's hand as he unlocked the unit. He shrugged her off and tugged her against him. It was ironic how one man could open doors that had once scared the hell out of her, while at the same time the man could be her safe haven.

He glanced down at her with a silent question in his eyes,

Are you ready? She filled her lungs with the scent of years gone by and nodded, though she didn't know if she'd ever truly be ready to go through her father's belongings.

Carson tightened his grip on her and lifted the door. The scrape of metal on metal grated on her already frayed nerves. His hand moved from her waist to her cheek, and he pressed a kiss to the top of her head.

"Several boxes, a file cabinet, and a leather recliner," Carson said stoically. "What do you want to do first? Take it in the ass as you bend over the boxes, or straddle me on the chair? Or maybe I'll sit in the chair and you can stand on the arms of it while I devour you."

She gave him her best deadpan look, and they both laughed. "Thank you. I needed that."

"Oh, you think I was kidding?" He gave her a chaste kiss. "Yeah, you're right. I probably was. But now that I'm thinking about your pretty little treasure above me—"

Her cheeks flamed. "Carson! They have cameras all over this place. They can probably hear everything you say."

He looked up and down the hall, a wicked grin spreading across his handsome face. "Let it be known," he announced loudly, "that I'd like to eat this woman until she screams my name so loud, the people in the next building will want my phone number."

She grabbed him by the collar and yanked him down until they were eye to eye. "Who are you, and where is my conservative-when-in-public friend?"

"He's too fucking happy that you're here with him to hold it in."

His mouth came coaxingly down over hers, kissing her until her legs turned to jelly and the rest of her body tingled with desire.

He drew back and brushed his thumb over her cheek. "I handle security for this place. Nobody's listening unless there's an issue and they need to revisit the videos." The edge of his mouth tipped up in a cocky smile. "Do you really think I'd share anything I do to you with anyone else?"

"No. But I do think you'd do all those things to me in this storage unit if you thought it would make it easier for me to handle going through my father's things." She went up on her toes and kissed him again, loving the freedom to do so. How did they get here overnight? Where kissing him like he was hers came so easily? She didn't know how, or why, they'd drawn those lines of secrecy in college about their relationship, and she'd never really questioned it back then. She'd liked the secrecy. It had been safe. Unfortunately, she had a feeling it had also increased the shame she'd felt about the things they did. But now wasn't the time to bring that up.

"Anything for you, baby." He not-so-discreetly adjusted his erection, and she giggled.

He scowled and trapped her against the wall, angling his body, blocking her from the camera. He pushed his hand into her jeans, sliding expertly over to her wetness like a heat-seeking missile. A gratified smile formed on his face. "It sure feels like you were just as affected as I was."

He thrust his fingers into her and she went up on her toes, giving him better access.

"Carson," she pleaded. Taking advantage, she groped him through his jeans.

He made a growling sound in the back of his throat, fiercely reclaiming her mouth, thrusting his tongue to the same rhythm as his fingers, taking her right up to the verge of madness. She focused on the enthralling tug in her belly, willing it to consume her. He grabbed the wrist of the hand she was taunting him with and held it above her head, grinding his cock against her as he continued his machinations beneath her panties. Her sex swelled around him. He pressed his thumb against her clit, kissing her harder. Bright lights exploded behind her closed lids as waves of ecstasy crashed over her. He continued his masterful torture through the very last of her climax, her body quaking against his hard frame.

When she finally came down from the peak he released her wrist and laced his fingers with hers, lowering her arm to beside her head and kissing her softly. She gasped as his fingers passed over her sensitive nerves. He brought them to his mouth and sucked them clean. Then he pulled her into his arms, rubbing the shoulder of the arm he'd held above her head.

"Now you should be a little less nervous," he said into her ear.

An aftershock trembled through her. "If you could bottle yourself, you'd be a millionaire. One dose can turn a woman inside out *and* calm her down."

"Babe, I passed *millionaire* a long time ago." He patted her ass. "Let's not forget, I don't share—bottled or otherwise. Got it?"

Oh yeah, she got it all right. She got it *good*.

A FEW HOURS later they'd gone through all but two of the boxes. It hadn't been as difficult as she'd expected, and she was sure it was because Carson was with her. He lightened the mood as they sifted through the things her father had thought worthy of keeping, like her science fair awards, report cards, pictures of her grandparents, and a mug she'd given him when she was a senior in high school. The mug had a picture of a chicken wearing glasses, sitting at a desk reading. A thought bubble above the chicken's head read, "When you don't know the answer, question the question." She remembered giving it to him for one of his birthdays, and he'd thrown the saying back at her throughout the years, just about every time she didn't know an answer. She missed him immensely and was glad Carson had offered to come with her.

She glanced down the hall where he was pacing, his cell phone pressed to his ear as he talked to Brett. Tawny stood by the window looking out over the city, thinking about how her father had led her back to Carson. She touched her forehead to the cold glass and closed her eyes, listening to the muffled cadence of Carson's voice. A few minutes later she heard his footsteps approaching. His arms circled her waist, and he kissed her neck, loosening the knots in her stomach.

"Are you holding up okay?"

"Mm-hm." She thought about the two remaining boxes, and trepidation swept through her. One was still sealed from when she'd packed it up after college, and the other had her mother's name written across the top in her father's messy handwriting.

Carson turned her in his arms. "You're nervous again."

He pulled down the collar of her sweater and kissed her shoulder. He was right there for her, soothing every emotionally jagged edge.

"A little," she admitted.

"We could take the last two boxes back to my place and you can go through them in private," he suggested.

"I'd like that. Besides, you probably have things to do while I'm here."

"I'll call Barton and have him pick them up. But as far as having something else to do, you've been out of my life for far too long. I've only got a few days with you, and I intend for us to spend every minute of them together. Brett agreed to handle things at the office."

"Are you sure? I don't want you to miss work or change your plans because of me."

"I'm positive, and we're going to start by getting out of here and doing things we never did together. Silly shit, because I want to hear you laugh."

"You always make me laugh."

"We've got a lot of years of laughter to make up for. Brett mentioned that my brothers are getting together to watch the football game tomorrow night at Dylan's." He pulled her in closer. "Since you blew me off nearly every time I asked you out in college, I figured we could meet up with them, unless you'd rather not."

"First, yes. I'd love to meet the rest of your brothers since I've only met Brett. And second…*blew you off?* You *never* asked me out."

"Seriously?" He looked at her like she was crazy. "You don't remember me suggesting we go to parties, or go out with a group of people? Or every damn Thursday night when I said we should grab dinner over the weekend?"

"*Pfft.* You never meant it like you're implying."

He stepped back with an appalled expression. "What's wrong with you? I meant it *exactly* like I am implying."

"Carson…?" She shook her head. He couldn't have meant it that way. Could she have misread his intent? "You had dates every weekend. Those were your hookup nights, and don't try to tell me they weren't."

His eyes narrowed, and his expression turned serious again. "I never *dated*. You know that."

"Whatever. *Dated. Hooked up. Fucked.* Whatever words you want to use, you were *busy*." Why did it still sting to think about that? "Before we ever started sleeping together, you told me that you could never be with just one woman. Don't you remember that?"

He ground his teeth together, pacing again. "Christ, Tawny. That was before we got together, when I thought my sexual needs would lead me astray. But then *you* happened, and everything changed. I didn't need anyone else. I would have turned them all away from day one for you, but you made it perfectly clear that you didn't want that with me."

She froze. "I...I don't remember it that way." *Holy cow.* Had she really led him to believe that?

He closed the distance between them. "You don't remember me telling you that none of those girls meant anything?"

"Sure, but—"

"You don't remember me telling you on Sunday nights, after we started sleeping together, that no one else existed in my head but you?"

She swallowed hard. "I thought that was just, you know, sex talk."

"I don't do 'just, you know, sex talk.' Those other girls didn't get that. They got nothing but cold, mechanical sex."

She laughed. "Now you're pushing it. You don't *do* cold, mechanical sex."

"Did you even know me at all back then?" He turned away, rubbing the back of his neck. Each frustrated movement drove her anxiety higher. When he faced her again, his eyes drilled into her. "I didn't have cold, mechanical sex with *you*. But with them?" He pointed out the window, his arm rigid, his jaw tense. "With *any* other women before we got together, or since? *None* of them got, or will ever have, what I shared with you. *Ever*."

All the starch left her body, and she slumped against the wall, too confused and upset to think straight. "But...you always said that what we did together is who you are."

"And?" he said angrily.

"And...I don't understand, Carson. If that's true, then how could you not be like that with other girls?"

He stalked over, boxing her in with his hands on the windowsill. He leaned down, meeting her eye to eye. "I have never lied to you, or tried to pretend I was something I wasn't. You know that. What we do together is who I am. The *real* me. Only you got the real me, Tawny. No one else."

"Okay," she said, still feeling blindsided by his confession of having wanted more with her.

He held her gaze, a flurry of conflicting emotions written in the tension around his mouth and the warmth in his eyes. "I always wanted more of you, but I respected you too much to push. And I was too proud to chase or beg, or whatever I would have had to do. I fucked all those women before you because I was a horny kid, and I stopped sleeping with them when we started sleeping together. But the hell with it, Tawny. I'll chase now. I'll chase *you*."

Tears welled in her eyes. He'd stopped sleeping with the other girls? Wasn't that what she'd always wanted? The answer was too confusing for her, because of how conflicted she'd been about the things they'd done together all those years ago. Would she have been as conflicted if they hadn't hidden their relationship? As she looked into his honest eyes, she realized that what she would have done back then didn't matter. All that mattered was what she felt for him now.

"I'm sorry," she said. "If you did ask me out and I blew you off, then maybe I didn't want to see it because I was afraid of other people somehow knowing what we were doing behind closed doors. I never even talked about sex with friends. I wasn't like you. I was never good in crowds. How do you think I would have been if someone found out and...I don't know...made a joke about it?"

"I never would have let that happen. I knew how careful and shy you were. Didn't you know that?"

She shrugged. "I was so confused back then..."

He uttered a curse and pulled her into his arms. "Damn it. We were young and oblivious to what mattered. I didn't even realize how deeply I cared for you until years later, when I was *still* comparing every woman I met to *you*, which is also messed up, because you broke me when you ended things because of a goddamn woman who meant nothing to me. I used to get through the week knowing that Sunday nights I'd have you in my arms again, like the payoff for behaving while we studied together. When you took that away because of some *nobody* I'd slept with two years earlier, it didn't erase my feelings. It just fucking hurt. You took a piece of me with you when we went back to being friends."

"I'm sorry. I'm so sorry." A tear slipped down her cheek with the memory of that night, of Carson offering the same explanation to her, but she'd been too overwhelmed and upset to listen. She had to make things right. If they had any chance of putting their missing pieces back together, she had to tell him the whole truth.

"That wasn't the reason," she said just above a whisper.

"What?" Confusion and anger stared back at her.

"I didn't end things because of that girl," she clarified.

"But—"

"I mean, that's what I said, but that wasn't the real reason. It was the easiest way out." She stared at his chest to keep from looking into his eyes while she revealed her shameful secret. "I was scared of who I was becoming. I was ashamed that we had this secret, which felt taboo *and* thrilling. It completely overwhelmed me. I couldn't even look at you without wanting to do dirty things together. It was too much. I felt like a sex addict but with these all-consuming emotions toward you." She spoke as fast as she could, unable to believe she was baring her soul after all these years, but he deserved the truth, and she wanted to finally say it out loud. "I couldn't pay attention in class, or when we studied together. And when I thought you were out with other girls? I nearly lost my mind. I was out of control. I—"

He tipped her chin up, forcing her to look into his compassionate eyes, bringing another onslaught of emotions.

"Jesus, Tabs. How could you keep that from me?"

"What was I supposed to say? 'Guess what, Carson? You know all those things I love doing with you? They make me feel like I've become an out-of-control pervert.'"

"Holy Christ," he seethed. "Is that what you think of us?"

"No!" She squeezed her eyes shut to stave off tears, and when she opened them, he was staring into her eyes. The man was not afraid of *anything*.

"Tawny, *why* are you here? Why did you come back if you feel that way?"

"Because I *don't* feel that way anymore." She swiped at her tears, and he took a step back, a skeptical look hovering in his eyes. "I haven't for a very long time. I married Keith because he was *safe*. He would never sleep with anyone else, or ask me to do anything even the least bit *creative* in the bedroom."

"I wasn't sleeping with anyone else." He crossed his arms over his chest, his biceps twitching.

"I know that *now*."

"What does that have to do with how you feel about what we did? Or why you're here now?"

"Because," she said too loudly, but she was unable to quiet the monsters she was finally setting free. "Don't you get it? I spent all those years with Keith trying to change who I was. I thought if I married someone safe, those urges that were so overpowering would go away, but they never did. I spent my marriage wishing I could feel *more*, love *harder*. Keith and I were like good friends and roommates who happened to sleep together, but it was nothing like what I'd experienced with you, even as a friend, without the sexual benefits. Even before you and I were sleeping together you were my everything, Carson. I felt lucky to have you as my best friend. There was no passion with Keith, nothing that made my heart pound."

She paced, trying to get her thoughts out as clearly as she could. "I bought sexy lingerie and made comments about heating things up in the bedroom, but that wasn't him, and I can't blame him for that. It was *me* who had the issue. You opened a door and I tried to force it closed, but it *wouldn't* close. It wouldn't close because I realized that what I missed, what I craved, has always been more than just passionate sex. It was *you*. You were always there in our bedroom, in my head, and Keith knew it. He knew I never stopped wanting you. I'm here because I've hit a wall, Carson. I can't move forward with my life. I'm stuck in this place with you in my head and in my heart, and I don't know if it's real or what to make of it. I have to get some perspective about us and what all these feelings mean. And before you say anything, I've grown up, Carson. I'm not that naive, introverted girl anymore. I *know* what we were doing wasn't wrong. And honestly, if it was, I don't care, because in the years since I ended things with you, I've felt even more out of control than I did before I ended it. Until now."

Relief washed over his face, followed by something more conflicted.

"I won't lie to you," she promised. "I'm still confused about things, but not about what we did together or my feelings about us. I'm just confused about where that fits in."

"Fits in with who? Or what?"

"I don't know. Maybe I am still naive in some ways. Does what we do have a name?" She tucked her hair behind her ear and focused on a vein in his arm as she spoke, concentrating on that so she didn't chicken out. "I went to one of those private BDSM clubs after I was divorced, right before I moved to Paris, to see if I could feel all those things I felt with you again. But it was all wrong. It felt dirty or something. Not *dirty*. I mean, I'm not judging those people. I know it's *me* that's messed up. I didn't even know how to do what they wanted me to do right. I felt like someone had poured pepper in a high-end fragrance, and I was the pepper. It was a terrible experience."

"*Christ almighty*," he uttered. "Look at me, Tabs," he said a little softer.

She met his gaze, expecting to see disappointment, or a look of repulsion, but the compassion in his eyes nearly brought her to her knees. He closed the distance between them again, and she ached to be in his arms.

"I wish you had talked to me. I hate that you went to that type of place looking to fill a void you never should have had." He clenched his teeth, and the muscles in his jaw bulged, but she sensed he wasn't angry with her. "You're not messed up, baby. I went through all those conflicted feelings before we got together. I could have helped you through it. I would have understood, and maybe then I could have convinced you to be with me more than just Sunday nights."

A tear slipped down her cheek. "I never knew you wanted that."

"I know. Damn it, if I had pushed, then we wouldn't have kept our relationship a secret, and maybe you would have felt differently." He scrubbed a hand over his jaw. "We can't change how we communicated back then, but we can change how we communicate starting right now. If you need to label what we did, call it making love *our* way. You didn't like that club because you are no more a submissive than I am a dom. We do what we feel, when we feel like it. There are no rules between us, no expectations, no right or wrong. Well, other than I will not share you." His lips curved up in a sexy smile, and she couldn't help but return it with a smile of her own.

"You shared yourself in college," she reminded him.

"I was a stupid kid, and that ended when we were together. I no longer make mistakes with my body." He brushed her tears away. "I promise you that if we're together, I will never touch another woman. But you have to make me a promise—"

"I'd never hook up with someone else." Her voice cracked, and she paused to try to gain control.

"I know you won't. That's not what I was going to say." The commanding look she knew so well returned, and when he spoke, his voice held the steel pierce of a demand. "If at any point you feel even an inkling of what you felt back then, you need to tell me right away. You can *always* talk to me."

Part of her was upset that they'd lost so many years together, while another part—a bigger part—thought she'd needed that time to grow up and figure out who she really was. But she still couldn't help wondering if she would have been happier figuring that out with Carson by her side.

"I know I can. I think I've always known that, but I was too…I don't know…*consumed* by it all? What I feel for you was—*is*—overwhelming."

His gaze softened, and his tone followed. "Are you scared now?"

She could no sooner withhold the truth from him than she could hide it from herself. "Yes and no."

He took both of her hands in his, rubbing his thumbs over them, comforting her in ways only he knew how. That simple motion, those little touches, his thumbs soothing over her hands, or when he cradled her face and brushed his thumbs over her cheeks, were the things he used to do when they were friends, before they became lovers. She'd fallen in love with him then, over sci-fi movies and Junior Mints, pizzas and textbooks, before they'd even shared a first kiss. Those things would always bring her back to the very soul of their relationship.

"Me too," he said. "But you're here now, and as long as you don't shut me out, we can figure it out together."

Chapter Five

UNDERSTANDING WHAT TAWNY had gone through in college was bittersweet. Carson *needed* honesty, and even with her confession, he felt she'd been as honest as she could have been back then. He knew better than anyone the way sexual urges could feel as paralyzing as they were empowering, and now that he understood what she'd gone through, he would take extra care to make sure she never felt that way again. No more hiding, no more easing up on his emotions. If she wasn't all in at the end of their time together, it sure as hell wasn't going to be because he'd backed off the way he had in college. He was going to love her the way she deserved to be loved, in public and behind closed doors. If anyone was going to get hurt, it would be him, and now that she was in his arms again, that was a chance he was willing to take.

"I never figured you for a cheap date," Tawny teased as they left a café, where they'd shared soup and sandwiches. Barton had taken them to drop off the remaining boxes at Carson's house, and then he'd dropped Carson and Tawny off at Bryant Park.

They headed for the Winter Village, a European-inspired open-air shopping area decked out with bright, colorful holiday lights, featuring artists from around the world. Each shop was housed in a custom-designed, glass-sided kiosk.

"Cheap my ass. I made reservations at One if by Land, Two if by Sea for dinner." Carson draped an arm over her shoulder as they moved through the crowd.

"Um...? Fish and chips?"

He stopped walking and tugged her against him, causing a wave of people to split around them like the Red Sea. "Do I seem like a fish and chips type of guy to you?"

"Well, you are really good at handling your *rod*."

Her eyes sparked with heat, and he lowered his mouth, stopping when they were a whisper apart. She fisted her hands in his coat and went up on her toes, trying to claim a kiss as he pulled out of reach.

Her green eyes narrowed, and she tugged his coat harder. "Give. Me. Those. Lips."

Damn, he loved when she got bossy. "Or else?"

"Or else..."

She searched his eyes, and he wondered if she knew that whatever it was didn't matter. He'd kiss her breathless for the rest of her life if she'd let him.

"Or else I'll withhold my body."

He slid his hands beneath her coat, thankful that it covered her ass, and grabbed just that, holding her against him again. "You sure you want to do that?"

Her breath left her lungs in one heated word—"*No.*"

"That's my girl. I'll have you know, One if by Land is rated as one of the most romantic restaurants in the *world*. I might want to have fun and date you like we should have done years ago, but I'm not going to treat you like a college kid. Not for dinner, and not in the bedroom."

She licked her lips, her eyes widening with his promise as he guided her out of the middle of the crowd.

He leaned in, placing his mouth beside her ear. This time he was going to make damn sure she knew exactly what he was thinking. "I unknowingly hurt you by holding back once, Tabs. I'm not going to make that mistake again."

He lowered his mouth to hers tenderly, pulling her tight against him, chest to chest, thigh to thigh, as he took the kiss deeper. She moaned, grasping at his shoulders, trying to take more of him, more of their passion. He'd always loved kissing Tawny, but kissing her in public like this blew his mind and filled him in ways he never thought possible. If he'd kissed her like this in public when they were in college, she'd have turned to dust out of sheer embarrassment. Man, he'd fallen so hard for *all* of her back then, her sweet vulnerabilities and her private sexual prowess. He never imagined his desires could run even hotter, that his emotions could soar higher. But when her hands moved softly around his neck, giving herself over to their kiss, he wanted to jump five steps ahead to being on his knees enjoying another part of her. Someone bumped his shoulder, knocking him out of his fantasy.

Carson kept hold of Tawny, glaring at the offender.

"Sorry, man," the guy said.

"No worries," Carson muttered, turning his attention back to Tawny. "You okay?"

"Yeah," she said breathily. "Your kisses have always made the rest of the world disappear. That's dangerous for me."

"I'm definitely going to use that to my advantage in the bedroom, but I'll try to be mindful in public."

"No, don't," she said quickly, her cheeks flushing. "I need this, Carson. I thought I'd learned everything I could about myself when we were apart, but I'm learning even more being with you."

They headed for the shops, and he kissed her again and again as they made their way through the crowds. He hadn't paid much attention to the holidays since college, when he and Tawny used to make a big deal about them before winter break. Now it was just another time of year, another good excuse to get together with family. But as he walked through the market with Tawny by his side, watching her admire handmade jewelry, books, artwork, and holiday ornaments, Carson felt the joy of the holidays approaching the way he used to, and his mind began to wander. He envisioned spoiling Tawny with lavish gifts, taking her away for a weekend at an exclusive resort, where he could pamper her away from the rest of the world. He glanced at her standing a few feet away, looking adorable as she sniffed scented candles, smiling at the ones she liked and wrinkling her nose at the ones she didn't. He could watch her all day long.

"What do you think?" He held up a holiday ornament of Mr. and Mrs. Claus kissing, imagining a Christmas tree in his house for the first time ever. The prospect of decorating it with Tawny and having her by his side when his family got together for Christmas dinner excited him. He knew he was getting miles ahead of himself, but he didn't care.

"Aw, that's cute. Do you put up a Christmas tree?" She picked up another candle and sniffed it. "Remember how we used to put up a tree weeks before Christmas and decorate it together?"

He laughed. "Yeah. That was fun, except when you made me drink eggnog, which is disgusting."

"It is not, but it was fun to watch you gag it down." She held up a candle. "I'm going to buy this."

He took it from her hands and read the label. "Cashmere?"

"It reminds me of you, and you didn't answer my question about a Christmas tree."

He loaded up his arms with *all* of the cashmere-scented candles and headed for the cashier.

"Carson…? What are you doing?"

"They remind you of me. I'm filling the house with them. I might stick one in your purse, in your coat pocket…" *And if you run back to Paris, I'm going to ship you a truckload.* The thought of her leaving festered in his gut like an open wound. He paid for the candles and the ornament, and they headed back out into the brisk air.

"I can't believe you bought them *all.*"

He chuckled as they went into an eclectic shop filled with handmade gloves, hats, scarves, and all sorts of small antiques. Tawny picked up a red child-sized scarf with reindeers on it, and a pair of matching mittens.

"Are those for someone you tutor?" he asked.

"No, although I am still tutoring at an orphanage. These are for a little girl named Adeline, who lives at the orphanage, but I don't tutor her. Not formally, anyway. I've been teaching her English, but that just sort of happened. I wasn't brought in to tutor her. She's five, and she's the sweetest, most precious child. We met when I first moved to Paris. She was three, and she'd lost her family in a fire. I'd just lost my dad, and it was helpful to have her to focus on. I read to her, played games. She was so shy, she reminded me of myself when I was younger, so it was easy to connect. We've been spending time together ever since."

There was something maternal in her eyes that reminded him of his mother when she spoke of him and his siblings. "I'm sure she'll love them. You should get a hat to go with it." He reached up on a shelf and found a white hat with reindeers and a red pom-pom. "Nobody likes cold ears."

"Thanks. That'll look beautiful on her. She's got long brown hair and big blue eyes."

She could have been describing Lorelei. "She sounds adorable."

"As all five-year-olds are," she said casually, but he could see by the way she gripped the goodies for Adeline that this little girl was special. She picked up a pair of thick, adult-sized mittens and lifted them to her nose, breathing them in.

"What are your plans, Tabs? You came a very long distance to have your way with me. Then what?"

"I guess that depends. I haven't had my way with you yet. You've only had your way with me." She rubbed the mittens over her cheek with a sultry look in her eyes.

"Is that so? Feeling lucky enough to play dice?"

Her cheeks pinked up, and damn, he loved that she still blushed over the word *dice*.

He stepped closer and took the mittens from her hands, feeling the luxurious material. "Someone still has a thing for cashmere." It just so happened he did, too.

She lifted her shoulder in a sweet and sexy shrug.

"I look forward to exploring that and to finding out what else you have a penchant for."

She pressed her hand to his chest and whispered, "I've never tried anything other than what we've done together."

"Then you have a thing for *me*, which is perfect, because my appetite is only for you."

They walked down the narrow aisle holding hands. He never imagined this would be enough, but he could spend all day talking and simply being with Tawny. Sleeping together had deepened their relationship, but in the two years prior, she'd been the bright light to his days. Whether they were studying or had headed into town for an afternoon didn't matter. She'd never been caught up in drama other women seemed to thrive on. Just being with her had calmed and centered him, filling all the lonely places inside him in a way his guy friends, or hookups, never had. But even with her acceptance of his public displays of affection, he wondered if those feelings she'd had about what they did behind closed doors would return.

"Do you still collect antique perfume bottles?" He reached for a bottle at the back of a shelf, and her eyes lit up.

"Yes, but it's more than a collection at this point." She took the bottle from him, cradling it as if it were liquid gold. "This is gorgeous, a René Lalique." She ran her fingers over the intricately carved figure of a woman, which formed the stopper. "Lalique started as a jeweler, and he used a casting process called *cire perdue*, which means *lost wax*. He'd hand-carve designs into wax, press them into clay to create a mold, and then melted—or *lost*—the wax so that molten glass could be poured in. It was genius. He used demi-crystal because it was inexpensive and easy to work with. The milky opalescence that you see in this bottle became his trademark."

He was entranced by the passion in her voice and the way she caressed the bottle like it was a treasure. He'd missed that, too. Most of the people he knew got caught up in how much they earned, their popularity in their field, and how soon they could retire. But whether it was schoolwork or tutoring, Tawny had always followed her passions rather than chasing a status.

"Oh gosh," she said with a nervous laugh. "I'm rambling. I'm sorry. It's the perfumer geek in me."

"I adore the perfumer geek in you. And now this bottle is

yours," he said.

"Carson, this has got to cost more than four hundred dollars. You don't need to buy me things. That's not why I came to see you." She straightened her spine and said, "I am a sought-after perfumer. I have *plenty* of money."

The pride in her eyes told him he was crossing a fine line, but he was going with his heart and not his head this time. "Honestly, babe, I don't think you *need* me for much of anything. I *want* to take you out to do fun things, enjoy nice dinners, buy you gifts, and cherish you in every sense of the word. You came all this way to try to understand what was between us so you could move forward, and I'm going to do everything within my power to show you that what you need to move forward is the man standing right in front of you."

She smirked and tucked her hair behind her ear. "So…you're *buying* my affection?"

"Pretty much," he teased. "You got a problem with that?"

She looped her arm in his as they walked through the shop. "Nope. You sure you're rich enough to handle me?"

"This, coming from the girl who wouldn't allow me to buy her a sweatshirt that day we got stuck in the library when it was snowing out."

She picked up a scarf and wrapped it around his neck, tugging him down toward her. "For a smart guy, you're really dense."

"That's not going to get you many presents." He kissed the tip of her nose.

"Do you remember what you did when I told you not to buy me a sweatshirt?"

He thought back to that blistery day. The snow had come on fast and had dumped several inches while they'd been studying. "I gave you mine."

She grinned and set the scarf back on the table, and he folded his arms around her, drawing her closer. "Looks like you weren't the only one who missed a few cues back then." He pressed his lips to hers. As they left the shop he said, "How about this time we don't chance miscommunication and try to use very clear sentences?"

"Okay." She bit her lower lip. "Carson, I *need* something."

Now we're talking. "Want to head back to my place?"

"No," Tawny said seductively. "I want to do it *here*." She raised her brows flirtatiously. "And I need it *bad*."

CARSON'S EYES DARKENED. "You've got my *full* attention."

Tawny motioned with her finger for him to come closer, then whispered in his ear, "I *need* hot chocolate with whipped cream."

His hearty laughter made her laugh, too.

He took her hand and led her toward another café. "Fair warning, whipped cream won't soothe the burn of hot chocolate licked off your body."

"I'm not worried," she said playfully. "The ice will help."

"Ice? That sounds interesting."

"You're taking me ice-skating."

"I am, am I? I don't know how to ice-skate," he said, holding the door to the café open for her.

She poked him in the stomach as she walked through. "Even better. The teacher becomes the student."

"Christ, what'd you do? Roll virtual dice I wasn't aware of?"

"Something like that."

After enjoying chocolate kisses and passing on sexy innuendos about whipped cream and all things warm and sweet, they made their way to the outdoor ice rink. They stowed their bags in a locker, and Carson scowled as he laced up his skates.

"Nervous?" Tawny asked.

He gazed up at her with an amused look in his eyes. "Do you remember the first time your hands and legs were bound to my bed?"

Her gaze darted around them, hoping nobody else had heard him. "Yes," she said quietly.

"What did it feel like?" he asked too matter-of-factly for such an intimate question.

She squirmed on the bench, adrenaline heating her cheeks as she gathered the courage to tell him the truth. She leaned closer and whispered, "I was excited and curious, but *really* nervous. I had never felt as exposed and defenseless in all my life. The only reason I didn't beg you to cut me loose was because I trusted you one hundred percent."

"Then you know exactly how I'm feeling right now." He whispered, "I'm in your hands, babe. I trust you."

She pushed to her feet, balancing perfectly on her skates. "My father taught me to skate when I was five. He said my mother had loved it, and that made me want to excel at it, too." She reached for him. "This time, I've got *you*."

He rose on wobbly ankles. Their eyes connected, and through the heat she saw that he'd picked up on her reassuring him with his own words.

As she led her hulking, brilliant man onto the ice, a new and unfamiliar sensation spread through her. She'd never felt as though Carson controlled or dominated her in any way she didn't enjoy or want, but leading him onto the ice, showing him something new and different, the way he had shown her in the bedroom, was invigorating. Maybe this, too, had been missing from their relationship in college. He'd always been the teacher in the bedroom. Even though he allowed her to lead once she felt comfortable doing so, she'd never had anything new to show him. There were still many pieces of their past, and her own feelings, that she didn't understand, but she was beginning to put the puzzle pieces together.

She skated beside him, holding his hand as he got used to the awkward feeling of standing on blades. "Try not to let your ankles wobble."

"Try not to struggle too much against the bindings," he retorted, playing off the first time she'd been bound to his bed.

"Exactly." She remembered almost every word he'd said to her that night, and she used them now. "'Relax. Let your body take over. Be in the moment with me.'"

The wickedness in his smile made her insides heat up. His long legs moved fluidly, though his ankles tilted inward.

"You're going to have sore ankles. Someone might have to rub them for you."

He raised his brows. "I think I'm going to like this skating thing."

He stumbled, and Tawny shifted swiftly, catching him before he fell, both of them laughing. She recited what he'd said when they'd first begun studying together—changing a few words to fit their new situation. "You've got a good grasp on this, but I think we could help each other get an even better understanding if we practiced together. I have the next few afternoons open if you're interested."

He pressed his lips to hers and hauled her against him,

wobbling unsteadily and clinging to her. "I'd like that very much. Think you can teach me like this?"

Only if you want to skate with a hard-on. "I'm willing to try anything once."

By their second time around the rink Carson was skating without any trouble. He was athletic and competitive, so she'd known he'd catch on quickly. The afternoon flew by in a whirlwind of laughter and kisses. Tawny couldn't remember ever being this happy or this at ease. As they walked the mile and a half to his house hand in hand, it began snowing. She tipped her face up toward the sky and opened her mouth, catching snowflakes on her tongue and feeling freer than she ever had. She'd noticed other women checking Carson out at the skating rink, and jealousy had prickled the back of her neck. She'd welcomed the sensation, because a much bigger revelation had hit her. And as snow melted on her tongue like secrets, she wanted to share the revelation with him.

"There are about a million dirty thoughts running through my mind right now," Carson said as he tugged her closer. "But you look so cute, I almost feel guilty thinking them."

"You think I'm cute?" She met his smiling eyes.

"I've always thought you were cute, Tabs. Cute, sexy, hot. Want me to keep going?"

"Yes," she teased. "You're all those things, too. There were *lots* of women checking you out today—"

He opened his mouth to speak, and she silenced him with a kiss.

"Don't say anything yet. It's not a complaint," she said. "At first I was jealous, but then this feeling came over me, like I'd spent my entire life half asleep and suddenly I was fully awake. It was definitely an epic moment, and it wiped out that jealousy so fast."

"You felt fully awake from being jealous? I could have made that happen ten years ago if you really like the feeling."

"Stop," she said, blinking snowflakes from her eyelashes. "I'm being serious. It happened when I was skating backward, when we were holding hands. You were looking at me like you used to look at me when we were in bed together. But we weren't in bed, and my entire being, my *mind*, *all* of me, just came together in this magical awakening."

She touched his cheek the way she knew he loved and gazed into his gorgeous dark eyes, her heart beating so hard she was sweating beneath her coat despite the cold air. Snowflakes wetted his cheeks and the tip of his aquiline nose and speckled his hair. The snow was falling harder now, as if the covers she'd been living under for the past decade were breaking into a million little pieces.

"I think this is what was missing back in school," she admitted. "I never realized how much I needed the freedom to be a real couple with you. I was too busy worrying about people seeing us together and connecting the dots to what we were doing behind closed doors, and I think that made me feel even more ashamed. This feels right, holding hands, kissing in public, and *not* worrying about the stupid *what-ifs* in my head that choked out any possibilities of us having more than our secret nights together. I know now that you hadn't wanted to hide our relationship, but back then, between trying to keep my head on straight for school and being consumed by enough sexual energy to light up the state…"

A warm smile curved his lips. "To light up the state, huh?"

"You know it's true. This has been the absolute *best* day of my entire life, Carson. And this thing between us feels so real and *possible*, it's scary."

"*Scary* is going through our lives trying to fill a void with people who don't fit. It's trying *not* to think about you year after year, knowing I'll never shake you for good," he said earnestly, causing her heart to tumble. "You've given us four days and five nights to sink or swim. It's the second chance I never thought we'd have, and I'm a hell of a swimmer, Tabs. I'll carry you from one end of the ocean to the other and back if that's what it takes. I was scared at first, and I'm still nervous on some level, because you might run away again. But for me, the *possibility* far outweighs the fear."

Chapter Six

LATER THAT EVENING, as Tawny dressed for dinner, Carson stood in the living room gazing out the balcony doors at Gramercy Park, one of the only private parks in Manhattan. He'd purchased the luxurious home because the view of the park had reminded him of Tawny. When they weren't studying in the library, their dorms, or eventually, their apartments, they'd spend hours on the grassy quad. Tawny had always loved the smell of the outdoors. She used to say that wind had a smell, and that it wasn't just the scents of the world it carried, that it had a unique fragrance all its own. He felt himself smiling with the memories of all the times he'd tried to decipher the scents she spoke of, but it was like she existed on a different plane and had access to things he didn't. He'd strived to bring her passion for scents into the bedroom, with scented oils and lotions. Watching her facial expressions change from intense concentration to that of pleasure as she took in the aromas, especially when she was blindfolded, had been a high in and of itself.

He watched the snow coming down in sheets, clinging to tree branches and settling heavily over the pavement and plantings. As much as he wanted to wine and dine her, he wasn't about to risk taking her out in this weather. He glanced down at his cashmere tie, dress shirt, and favorite pair of alligator loafers.

Wining and dining doesn't have to take place at a restaurant.

He phoned the restaurant, and then he called Barton and made arrangements for dinner to be delivered.

He'd heard Tawny's phone ring, and the sound of her muffled voice filtered into his ears. He wondered who she was talking to. He wasn't used to the jealous feeling trying to claim him. Unwilling to entertain thoughts of her and any other man, he pushed aside the jealousy as quickly as it had come on. Many things about Tawny were still a mystery, but he knew he didn't have to worry about her seeing anyone else. He was moving carefully, easing into their sensuality, and it was killing him. But this time had to be different. Her love for him had to surpass her worries. He wanted to address her every fear and settle them. Even though each new discovery so far had deepened his love for her, he wasn't fooling himself. He knew that navigating their new relationship, and the last decade, would be like finding their way through a labyrinth, full of as much happiness as unexpected trouble and dead ends. But Carson had never believed there was only one means to an end, and he was determined to find their way together, even if it meant blazing a trail through uncomfortable territory.

With a hopeful inhalation, he went to the kitchen, gathered place settings for dinner, and carried them to the living room coffee table. They'd never been dining room table type of people. He turned on the fireplace and tossed a few pillows onto the floor to sit on. After he finished setting the table, he lit two of the candles they'd purchased earlier in the day. *It reminds me of you.* He opened the armoire in the corner of the room, revealing a large-screen television, turned on the stereo, and set the remotes on the mantel in case Tawny wanted to curl up and watch a movie.

He turned at the sound of heels on hardwood, catching sight of Tawny descending the stairs in a sexy little black dress, dark stockings, and a pair of sky-high heels. He was struck speechless. She was always beautiful, but tonight her strawberry-blond hair shimmered against the dark fabric, and she'd done something mystifying with her eyes, giving them a smoky, seductive appearance.

She ran her hands nervously over her dress as she stepped into the room, bringing her exquisite beauty into full view. The top of the dress was sheer across her breastbone and between her breasts, exposing an enticing path of braless cleavage. The wide neckline left a decadent expanse of bare shoulders for him to devour.

He placed a hand on her hip and brushed his cheek over hers, her exotic scent luring him in. "You look, and smell, incredible."

"Thank you. As do you." She glanced down at her heels. "I just saw the snow. I didn't think to bring boots."

"It's coming down really hard. I canceled our reservations and I am having dinner delivered. It should be here any minute."

She exhaled a shaky breath. "Okay. I still can't believe I'm here with you. I was so nervous when I was getting ready, it was like we were going out for the first time or something."

"We are, because everything is different now. There's no hiding, and even though we have history, we're starting over with clearer communication and a world of experience behind us. We won't make the same mistakes again, Tabs. We might make new ones, but we'll figure them out together."

Dinner arrived, and they sat on the pillows, feeding each other bites of steak and scallops, toasting their new relationship, and catching up on all the things they'd only touched on.

"You said your collection of perfume bottles had turned into something more," he said as he fed her the last of the scallops. "What did you mean?"

"I forgot you had the ability to remember every word I ever said." She finished her drink, and Carson got up to fix them each another. Tawny tucked her legs elegantly beside her and toed off her heels. "In my spare time, I've been coming up with fragrances inspired by emotions and feelings, and surprisingly, it all started with the unique elements of the bottles. I envisioned my own fragrances in them and started thinking about what perfumes I'd fill them with. It's sort of become an obsession of matching bottles with feelings and emotions and finding the right combination for each. The scents I've come up with are a bit too offbeat for the company I work for, but they speak to *me* on every level. I haven't been able to shake the feeling that I should do something with them." She tucked her hair behind her ear, her eyes slipping away for a moment. "Silly pipe dreams," she said softly.

"Silly dreams often lead to the most amazing outcomes. You know that."

"I'm not a risk taker, Carson," she said as they finished eating.

"You've never been a whimsical person, but you've taken risks. You risked everything when you broke it off with me and married Keith. You did what you felt you needed to, and you thought the risk was worth the outcome. But it was still a huge risk. You took another risk when you got divorced and moved to Paris. And now you're *here*, taking the biggest risk of all. Maybe they've all been calculated risks, but they're still risks. Talk to me, Tabs. I want to know what you're thinking."

"I guess I've been toying with the idea of doing something more personal. But I've got a secure job that pays me more than I could ever wish for, and giving that up would be..." She bit her lower lip and shook her head. "I don't know. Irresponsible? Stupid?"

"Or brilliant?" he suggested. "Tabs, I know nothing about the fragrance industry, but I *know* you. You've got the world's best smeller in that perky little nose of yours."

She laughed, and looked away with the compliment.

"What are you afraid of? Do you need capital?"

They carried the dishes into the kitchen as she explained. "No. Between my father's life insurance and what I've earned over the years, I've got plenty of money. But there's a lot to it. I'd need a small lab, retail space. And what I want to do is different and it might flop."

She turned on the faucet, and he reached around her and turned it off, placing several kisses along her shoulder. "I'll take care of the dishes later. I want to spend time with you and hear about your plans."

"The kitchen *is* a dangerous place for us." She dragged him by the collar out of the kitchen and across the living room to the balcony doors. "This is safer."

She looked gorgeous against the blue hue of the snowy night. His arms circled her from behind, and he couldn't resist tasting her shoulder again. "Tell me more. Figuring out what this is between us was important enough for you to take that risk. Are the fragrances you're creating and the enjoyment or fulfillment you get from them worth the risk?" He moved to her other shoulder, trailing kisses all the way to her neck.

"I don't know. I hope so, the same way I hoped seeing you would help me figure out how to move forward." She pressed her fingertips to the glass door, as if she needed it for stability. "If you keep kissing my shoulders, I won't be able to think straight."

He pressed his lips to the base of her neck, feeling her shiver against him. "Sure you can. Let's talk about striking out on your own. You must have been thinking about it for a long time, just as you've been thinking about me." He nipped at her neck.

"I can't," she said breathlessly, craning her neck to the side. "I told you your kisses undo me."

He flattened one hand on her belly and ran his other hand down her hip. "Concentrate," he whispered, knowing he was driving them both crazy. "I want to know how long you've been thinking about opening your own shop. I'll stop kissing you so you can talk."

She inhaled a shaky breath and spoke in a tremulous voice. "I've inquired about some small shops in Paris over the last few weeks, but more out of a what-would-it-take moment of insanity than anything else." She swallowed hard, and he tightened his grip on her.

"It's not insanity to want to make your dreams come true. You're a smart woman, and I'd bet you've been contemplating it for much longer than you're letting on. What's holding you back?" Not kissing her was killing him, but a drive to succeed had always been something they'd had in common, and he wanted to reconnect on every level, not just in bed.

"I came up with the idea a few years after college, but Keith thought it was too much of a long shot, which fed into my careful nature, so I tried to put it behind me. But the more I thought about it, the more I wanted it. And after my dad asked me about regrets, thoughts of you and ideas about opening up a perfumery got tangled up in my head, and neither one would let me be."

"Because you knew I'd support your dreams."

"I don't know. Maybe. You always understood my need to get top grades and study until I was bleary eyed. Or maybe I'm just being stupid, clinging to ideas that could never come to fruition."

"Don't fool yourself, Tabs. You didn't just want top grades. You wanted to know *more* than everyone else. I loved that about you. And that's what will make your own shop a success."

"I never said I *was* opening a shop. It's just an idea I've played with. It's a huge endeavor. And I wouldn't try to become the next Christine Nagel, although it would be nice to create the next Miss Dior Chérie or Dolce & Gabbana's The One for Her, but that's not my motivation."

"No?" He wasn't sure he believed that. Even if she didn't realize she wanted to be known in the industry on a broader spectrum, he knew that one day she would—and he wanted that to come true for her.

"*If* I did it," she said carefully. "And that's a huge *if,* so don't get your hopes up, I wouldn't want to commercialize and sell mass products. I'd want to create and sell my own fragrances in a small, boutique perfumery. I want to make fragrances based on individuals, who they are, what they love, the aura they give off. I want to make personalized perfumes and colognes that are lasting and unique, that remind lovers of what they adore about each other, and about themselves."

She leaned back against his chest, and he saw her smiling in her reflection in the glass.

"Nobody's doing it, Carson. There are create-your-own perfumes, but people hardly ever wear the right scents for their bodies. I have visions of a small shop where I spend time with

clients to determine what their perfect fragrance should be."
Her voice escalated with her excitement. "It's a crazy idea. I
mean, some fragrances have to go through hundreds of
renditions before they're perfected. I can't imagine I'd make any
profit given the time it would take. But it feels so right. Like it's
within my grasp and refuses to be ignored. The way you've been
all these years."

"Tabs, how can you doubt this? Don't you hear the excitement in your own voice? Feel it in your body?" He took her
hand and placed it over her heart, his mind racing with ideas
and connections. "Feel that? That's telling you this is right. But
you'll need an exclusive customer base that recognizes, and can
afford, the value of your products. I know a jeweler who works
in a similar fashion. I can connect you with him to pick his
brain, and maybe you can market to the same clientele. It's a
risk, but wealthy people love customized things, from cars and
clothes to *fragrances*, I'd bet."

"That's a big, fat *bet*, Carson. I'd imagine it would take
most of my savings to start a business like this, and who knows
how long it would take to gain clients." She sighed. "Besides,
I've been walking a safe path for years. It's all I know."

"It helped you become stronger, more focused, *and* realize
you'd made a huge mistake giving up the only man on earth
who is good enough for you."

She laughed. "There is *that*."

"You're so passionate about what you want to do. I think
you should give this serious consideration. I'll help you get
started, introduce you to the right people. Life is too short to do
anything you're *not* passionate about."

"You make it sound like such a simple decision. Thank you
for offering. I'll think about it." She fell silent for a minute, and

when she spoke, her voice was as soft and strong as the wine. "I'm passionate about you."

He pressed a kiss beside her ear, down her neck, and her back sank into his chest. "I'm passionate about you, too, Tabby."

"I love when you call me that."

"I know." His hand moved along her thigh, his fingers trailing over lace and the illicit bump of a garter. "Mm. That's *nice*." He wanted to talk more, but knowing she had on sexy lingerie made him harder by the second. He gathered her hair to the side and placed openmouthed kisses on her neck. "Give it serious thought, babe. You should do it."

She reached behind her, grabbing at the back of his legs. "Carson—"

"What, babe?" He squeezed her thigh, the heat of her center radiating over his fingers.

"I...I have other ties to Paris now," she said. "The children at the orphanage."

He brushed his fingers over her damp, hot panties.

"They...*Carson*," she whispered.

"Tell me," he said firmly, quickly losing grasp on his control. "I want to know."

"They're important to me," she said quickly.

He stilled, anxiety and love mounting inside him. He remembered when they were in college, she'd told him that over the summers she'd continued visiting the children she'd tutored. Tawny's heart was endless, and he couldn't imagine asking her to leave children she'd bonded with. "Then you're definitely going back?"

"I have a job there, a life, no matter how small."

"I know, baby, and your world is significant to me. Not

small in any way. What are we doing, Tabs? You came to me. I want you."

She turned in his arms and looked at him for a long, silent moment, a tangled web weaving between them.

"I don't know what I'm doing, Carson. I'm here to try to figure that out."

The vulnerability in her voice made his heart ache.

"We have to figure it out together," she said as she unbuttoned his shirt.

She set her smoky eyes on him, holding his gaze as she kissed the skin she revealed. It was all he could do to watch her loving him the way she used to as he silently worked to unweave the tangles. His company worked internationally. He could spend time in Paris, but he couldn't be there full-time. While he wrestled with the complications of a long-distance relationship, Tawny watched him intently. She opened her mouth, then closed it again, as if she were afraid to say something.

"Talk to me, Tabs. Don't hold it in."

"I'm not holding it in this time. I promise. It's just…How can I know what I'm going to do next when you own half of the decision?"

He clenched his jaw, a war raging in his head as Tawny tugged the tails of his shirt from his pants. He grabbed her hands. They were so small, so delicate, he craved the feel of them all over his body. With a fierce look of determination, she used all her strength to manipulate her hands within his and pressed her palms together.

"Help me decide, Carson. Take me like you used to. Let's see where we end up."

Christ, she may think he owned half of her decision, but she was so fucking wrong. She owned *him*, mind, body, and soul.

He would give her anything she wanted, anything she needed—and she clearly needed this. His chest constricted with the realization of what she was asking. They were on the exact same page, needing to see if she'd really grown past the uncomfortable feelings she'd described and whether she could handle doing what she craved without panicking the next day when they were out in public. She was testing her own boundaries, and he prayed she'd pass.

"Turn around," he commanded.

CARSON THREADED HIS fingers into Tawny's hair, tugging it to one side, clearing the way for his hot mouth. Her heart raced as he devoured her neck like he hadn't tasted her in forever, sucking and biting just hard enough to sting. She inhaled sharply, arching away from the sting and craving it at once. She flattened her palms against the cold glass, grinding against him. His hands moved roughly over her breasts, between her legs, lingering there.

"My baby wants this," he said hungrily.

"I've always wanted you."

She felt restraint in his touch as he slowed his efforts, his fingers moving in a mesmerizing pattern along her inner thigh, brushing lightly over her panties, then moving away again. He was a master at building anticipation, and *oh* how she'd missed this. She pressed her palms harder into the glass as he repeatedly slid his fingers along the seam of her panties, following it up to her hip, then down to the crest of her thigh. She closed her eyes as her breathing, and his hips, found the same rhythm as his hand. *Up, down, up, down, grind, thrust, grind, thrust.* The seductive beat pounded through her, anticipation burgeoning inside her until she thought she might explode. His hand stilled on her inner thigh, his chest pressed tightly to her back, as he sucked her earlobe between his teeth, and she heard herself moan. He didn't move, didn't breathe, just stayed right there, making her sex throb. Seconds ticked by in this position. The heat of his fingers against her skin, his teeth clamped on her sensitive earlobe. She was afraid to move, and at the same time, she *needed* to grind her hips, to feel his hardness moving against her. When he finally slid his fingers beneath her panties, dragging slowly over her slickness, her breath rushed from her lungs. She felt her entire body opening to him like a flower to the sun, willing him to enter her. She rocked forward with the hopes of those thick fingers taking her up on her offer, but the moment she rocked, he pulled free and ran his damp fingers over her thigh and garter.

"You dressed for me," he said in a guttural voice, thick with lust.

"For us."

He pressed a tender kiss to her shoulder. Then he stepped back, leaving her trembling against the assault of cooler air rushing over her heated flesh. She closed her eyes, shivering and wanting, listening to his steady breathing somewhere behind her. Her fingers curled against the glass, wishing they were curling into *him*. She heard the swish of his slacks as he moved behind her. Her body shook almost violently, and just when she thought she'd detonate from anticipation, she felt the press of his fingers on her back as he unzipped her dress and pushed it down her arms. It fell to her feet. Hot hands clutched her hips, helping her step out of the dress, and then his hands were gone again, and she was naked, save for her panties, stockings, and garters.

She opened her eyes, watching his reflection in the glass as he picked up her dress and laid it across the back of a chair. He stripped off his slacks, leaving on his shirt and tight, dark briefs. *Oh Lord*, he was going to tease her to no end. His body heat preceded him, washing over her back as he stood motionless behind her, letting her know he was there. He was in control. And he would not be rushed. Her sex clenched with need, and her nipples burned. What felt like forever, but in reality was probably only sixty seconds later, his breath coasted along her shoulder, and his tongue followed. He sank his teeth into her skin, and she gasped at the piercing pain and pleasure radiating through her core. His large, strong hands gripped her hips again and moved tightly up and over her rib cage. His thumbs brushed the sides of her breasts softly. She held her breath so she wouldn't miss it. She'd longed for this delicious torture, and Carson was an expert at doling it out, making her want him so badly she was already close to orgasm.

His hands moved to her ass, squeezing and caressing. His strong fingers pushed between the two globes, teasing all the way down to her slick heat, then back up again, wetting her skin. She couldn't suppress a moan, and his hands stilled. She squeezed her eyes shut, willing him on, never knowing if her reactions would garner more of his touch, or if he'd pull away, claiming *complete* control. She didn't want to know. She just wanted to experience him. When his hands slid south again, her breath rushed from her lungs.

"Did you forget how much I love your ass?" he asked in a husky voice.

How could she forget? She loved when he touched her everywhere, with his hands, his mouth, his *cock*. "I counted on it."

"Damn, baby." He pressed his rigid cock against her ass. "I *ache* to be inside you."

Oh God, yes.

He stepped away again, bringing another rush of cold air over her damp skin and sending shivers down her spine. She listened to the slide of fabric against skin, watching Carson's reflection in the glass as he removed his tie and shirt. He laid his tie over his shoulder and turned her toward him, holding his shirt in one hand, all his glorious muscles on display. Heat and desire spread through her, filling her lungs, her veins, the far reaches of every limb.

He tipped her chin up and brushed his lips over hers. "You are everything to me, Tabs. I need you to know that before we go any further."

She swallowed hard at the thunderous emotions surging through her. "I know."

He lifted her wrists and kissed her palms, his smoldering gaze darkening. "Touch me."

She lifted shaky hands to his face as he leaned down and claimed her mouth. The first touch of his lips was electric. Her fingers moved over his corded neck muscles, tight from restraint. He smelled of lust and greed and something much more intense. She caressed his cheeks and pushed her fingers through his short hair. He deepened the kiss, moaning his appreciation as she explored his shoulders and his hard, bulbous biceps. She arched forward, pressing her body against as much of him as she could and earning a heady groan from Carson. His tongue swept over hers, strong and sensual. His hand traveled over her back, into her hair. She waited for the sting of his grip, but as he used to do when they were making love, he held her expectations at bay. His hands moved down her torso again. She went up on her toes, seeking more, and he tore his mouth away, leaving her panting.

He took her hands in his with the look of deep concentration and dark seduction she hadn't seen in so many years it made her head spin, and somehow it also felt as familiar as if she'd looked in a mirror. She watched him meticulously align the sleeves of his shirt along the front panels, folding it until the width met some calculation in his brilliant mind, before using his shirt to bind her wrists. She remembered what he'd said to her the first time he'd bound them. She'd been so nervous, she could barely breathe, even when he'd said, *You're in control, Tabs. You're always in control.* She'd thought he'd meant because he would stop whenever she wanted him to. But she'd learned that there was an immense sense of control and freedom that came from surrendering completely to the person she trusted most. It seemed strange to her now, that the very thing that had empowered her had also broken her down.

She pushed those memories away as Carson moved swiftly, concentrating on the fold of the material, making sure it was flat against her skin. He was always careful with her, and she loved that about him. The warmth of the fire sailed over her already heated skin, heightening her arousal. She closed her eyes as he finished his task, anticipation stacking up inside her, seeping into every crevice, consuming her thoughts. She felt Carson adeptly unhooking the straps on her garter, sliding off her panties, and helping her step out of them. She opened her eyes, her knees weakening at the lust pooling in his eyes as his hands climbed up her legs. He slowed to run his thumbs along her inner thighs, stopping short of her sex. She gritted her teeth against a whimper trying to escape, and his eyes locked on hers.

"Close your eyes, Tabby."

She did, and Carson's intoxicating scent mixed with another, barely noticeable aroma. The first touch of the buttery-soft material to her eyes made her heart skip. *Cashmere.* She felt him fixing the tie into one of his special knots on the side of her head. *Never behind your head when you're lying down,* he'd once explained. *I want you to be comfortable.*

Her pulse sprinted, her vision now blocked by his tie. Then she was in his arms, her body pressed against his chest, breathing him in as he carried her and laid her on the sofa. When he lifted her bound hands above her head, she felt like her lungs opened completely for the first time in years. He spread her legs, the cushions dipping as he settled between them. On his knees? She assumed so as she felt the back of the couch move, like he was using it for balance. His mouth closed over her breast all at once, wet and hot, sharp teeth grazing over the sensitive peak. She gasped, and he pushed her breasts together, moving from one to the other, giving each a slow, hard suck. When he released them, he pinched one nipple, his mouth claiming the other, sucking so fervently she felt it between her legs. She arched beneath him, squirming with the titillating sensations searing beneath her skin. Then his mouth was on hers, rough and demanding. Instinct brought her bound hands up, and he flattened his palms over the underside of her arms, pushing them down again, pressing them into the cushions. His mouth left hers, and her eyes darted futilely beneath her blindfold as she felt him rising, hovering over her, his body heat radiating like the blazing sun. His tongue slicked along the underside of her arm, teasing the sensitive skin she might never in her entire lifetime have noticed if not for their sexual explorations. Heat slithered like snakes through her core, pooling between her legs.

She opened her mouth to beg for more, and he brushed his

chest over her mouth. She opened wide, licking and panting, needing so much more. His chest hair tickled, his nipple moved over her cheek, along her chin, as she tried anxiously to capture it. He rose, bringing a wave of cooler air over her skin, his hands still trapping her arms above her head. She felt the weight of his stare, heard the even cadence of his breathing, and when he lowered himself over her again and slicked his tongue along her other arm, her hips lifted off the cushions.

"Taste me, Tabby." Ragged desire laced his demand as his nipple brushed over her lips.

She didn't taste. She *devoured*, sucking his nipple, biting down the way he liked. His hips bucked, grinding deliciously against her center. He kept her arms trapped above her head, groaning as he crushed his chest to her mouth. When he rose, she whimpered, missing the weight of him, the taste of his salty skin. His mouth captured hers, one hand still holding her arm, kissing her so deeply her thoughts fragmented. Then he cradled her face, like he couldn't get enough of her, the way he used to. Sometimes they'd barely made it into his apartment before he'd grabbed her and kissed her that way. Not once in nearly two years as lovers had he stopped doing that, and now, in the height of passion, she realized how desperately she'd missed it.

"Three days," he said between kisses. "Three days left to make you mine."

Yes. The word lodged in her throat as he seared a path of openmouthed kisses directly to her sex. He pushed her legs open wider, and she felt his breath moving over her center. She felt exposed and *whole* and couldn't imagine how both were possible, but she couldn't pick that apart. Not when her heart was open and accepting for the first time in forever. She lifted her hips, and Carson held them down, forcing her to remain in the heady space of neediness, enduring his masterful seduction at the pace *he* desired. She lay panting, every nerve a live wire, aware of the plush cushions beneath her, the ache in her shoulder joints, the waves of heat the fire threw over her skin, and most of all, the love she felt emanating from Carson.

In the next breath, his tongue teased along the length of her sex in one tantalizingly languid move. She blinked against the blindfold and closed her eyes as his talented tongue circled her clit, around and around, then pressed hard, alighting throbs of desire. This became a mind-numbing pattern of licking, teasing, and pressing, until she was shaking and moaning, struggling against his hands stretched between her hips and thighs, keeping her open and holding her still. Darts of ice and heat traveled up her legs, and a string of pleas tore from her lungs. *This* was what she craved. *This* was what she needed. Electrified nerves, a lapse of her synapses, Carson's strong hands taking control, his mouth catapulting her up, up, *up*, until she could barely breathe.

She fisted her hands, straining against her bindings. An orgasm hung just out of reach. Then his mouth left her, and she cried out, "Carson, *please*—"

One hand released her, the other remaining in place, reminding her he was still in control. She heard ice cubes clinking against glass and bit her lower lip, her eyes following the sound even though she couldn't see. The cushions dipped, then rose, and dipped again, farther away. Then the shock of ice on her sex caused her body to clench, and she whimpered with the burn searing into her. Just when she didn't think she could take it anymore, he drew back, and her breath rushed from her lungs. He must have had the ice in his mouth, because his hands held her leg and hip once again.

He rubbed the ice along the crease between her thigh and her sex, around her swollen lips, then down the center of her slick heat. Every touch was pure pain and shock, despite the anticipation, but it quickly turned to scintillating pleasures. Cold liquid dripped over her hot skin as the ice melted, and he pushed his fingers deep inside her, making her hotter, wetter, and brought the ice to her clit. She bowed off the cushions, wanting his mouth to engulf her.

She tried to beg for more, but every muscle, every nerve, was focused between her legs. He was relentless, swirling the ice as his fingers invaded her, stroking over the spot that made her dizzy. He dragged the ice cube up the center of her body and rubbed it over her mouth. The scent of him, and her arousal, surrounded her. His cock ground between her legs, hot and thick, warming the frigidness away. He circled her nipple with the frozen cube, causing her breasts to flame and sting and pucker so tight they prickled.

"Carson," she pleaded.

He moved lower again, dragging the ice down her body and leaving it in her navel like a secret treasure. Her hips undulated, her body vibrating from the overwhelming sensations. When he slicked his tongue along her sex, a long, loud moan escaped. Then her nipple was between his finger and thumb, rolling deliciously, as he withdrew from her sex and teased over her ass. In the next breath he was feasting on her sex, and his finger pushed into her bottom at the same moment he squeezed her nipple. Her eyes slammed shut against a thousand crackling explosions beneath her skin, shooting all the way to the tips of her fingers and toes. A string of indiscernible noises sailed from her lungs.

Just when she started to catch her breath, he did it again,

and she shot right back up to the peak again, her body electri-fied. She should have expected the next assault, and the *next*, but each time he penetrated deeper and it was more thrilling than the last. He groaned as she lingered in orgasmic bliss and fell limply to the cushions. She was vaguely aware of him moving, but her mind was too scattered to focus on anything other than collecting every sensation as if she were a hoarder.

She felt his lips on her cheek, tender and loving. The gentle scratch of his whiskers. He knelt beside her, his hand brushing over her hair, his lips touching her forehead. He traced the ridge of her brow, her cheek, and jaw bones. He removed the tie from her eyes, and she blinked several times, trying to adjust to the dimly lit room and make her mind function again. The love and need in his eyes collided, bringing tears to hers. Oh, this man, her glorious lover and friend. They were so connected, the anchor to each other's storms.

"There you are," he whispered. "Still with me, baby?"

She managed a nod, or at least she thought she did. He lowered her arms slowly, unbinding her hands, and then she was in his arms again, cradled in his lap on the floor beside the couch. He was so big, his thick knees bent, holding her against his muscular body, and yet even with all those hard edges, he was soft and comforting.

He rubbed her shoulders and wrists, whispering between tender kisses. "You are the very air I breathe, Tawny Bishop. The grounding force that allows my world to make sense."

She felt like she'd flown into a dream, and she didn't want to wake up. She wrapped her arms around his neck as he rose to his feet. He blew out the candles, turned off the fireplace and stereo, and carried her upstairs. He stripped back the blanket of his luxurious bed and laid her in the middle, carefully removing her garter and stockings. She was too blissed out to move.

"I've missed you, Carson," she whispered.

His lips curved up, as if he'd seen it in her eyes before she'd said a word.

He stripped out of his briefs, unleashing his thick, eager cock, awakening every ounce of her again. She reached for him as he settled between her legs. She wanted to do so many things with him, *to* him, but as he came down over her, none of her urges were stronger than the need to love, and be loved by, him.

Leaning on his forearms, he cradled her head between his hands, looking at her like she was his only thought. She was aware of everything—the scent of her arousal on his skin, his chest hair tickling her breasts, his thighs pressing down on hers, the broad head of his cock nestled at her entrance, and the inescapable love in his warm brown eyes.

"What do you see, *Tabby*?" he asked.

"You, Carson. The *real* you. The one I never should have run from."

Chapter Seven

CARSON AWOKE BEFORE dawn to the feel of Tawny's fingers following the line of his spine down his back. A smile tugged at his lips, but he willed himself to remain absolutely still, curious to see what she did next. As still as he *could*, considering her thigh rested on his hamstring and her naked body was pressed against his side. He couldn't control his cock stiffening against the mattress. She kissed his side, as light as a feather, her fingers tracing the curve of his ass before they began a slow glide north again. Her lips touched him again and again, and her palm flattened over his ass, squeezing gently. She caressed his hamstring, her fingers diving deeper between his legs. This time when they moved upward, she dragged them over his balls, and they tightened beneath her touch. He ground his teeth together to keep from moving, but he felt her breathing quicken and knew she was aware of his arousal. She climbed over him and lay on his back, her cheek resting between his shoulder blades. Her hands ran along his biceps. He spread his fingers, welcoming hers as they laced together, and she exhaled a long dreamy sigh.

"Can I lay here forever?" she asked.

He heard the smile in her voice and brought their joined hands to his mouth, kissing each of her knuckles. "Baby," was all he could manage. Forever sounded damn good to him.

"I know I've said this too many times, but I missed you so much, Carson, I ache with it. I just want to lie here and soak you in."

He closed his eyes, reveling in her in the same way. They'd made love twice last night, and Tawny had fallen asleep in his arms with the most beautiful, peaceful smile on her lips. The tremor of nervousness he'd sensed in her since she'd arrived was gone. Her heart beat steady and sure against his back as she pressed a kiss there, and then another and another. God, how long had he waited for this, dreamed of it. Loving Tawny Bishop had felt like the unachievable. And here she was, in his bed, *soaking him in*. If he died right then, he would die a happy man.

"Tell me something about you I don't know," she said. "We've been talking about me since I arrived, and I want to know more about you. I want to know if you're happy. Do you enjoy your business as much as you hoped you would?"

"I do, Tabs. Cyber security, closing loopholes, solving puzzles, it's everything I'd wanted. When Brett joined me, it made the company even better. He's a smart-ass, but he's a good man, and the heavy hand in the partnership. When he came on board, we began handling private security for pop stars and celebrities. It's more than I could have hoped for. We've got plenty of connections to help you start your business."

"Stop acting like my starting a business is a given. There's a lot to consider." She kissed the back of his neck. "How are you still single, Carson? You must have your pick of women, and yet you let me walk into your life and I didn't have to wait in line."

He opened their joined hands and kissed her palm. "Because the one I wanted wasn't available." He closed their hands again. "It's always been you, Tabs."

"But do you date? I mean, you're such a passionate man. There must be women in your life."

"Nothing has changed since college in that regard. I don't date. I have a few women I see from time to time to blow off steam, but you don't really want to talk about them, do you?"

"No," she whispered, and scooted higher, her soft curves sliding against him. "For smart people, we were pretty dumb to let so much get in our way. I was dumb. It's really my fault."

"It was both of us. We were young and stupid," he said. "But smart enough to have found each other in the first place."

"I guess. And you fulfilled your dream, Carson. You always said you wanted to become an international security expert."

"I said I wanted to become the *best* international security expert," he corrected her. "And I am."

"What*ever*." He felt her smile as she kissed his neck again. "That's only because I didn't go into your field and blow you away."

"Well, you did *blow* me," he said playfully.

She laughed. "Did you know…" She paused, reminding him of all the times she'd led with those words when they were studying together and she knew more about a subject than he did. "Only six percent of people fulfill their childhood dreams? And only thirty percent of people work in what they'd consider their dream job or a related job. How can the statistics be so low?"

"I think a better question is *why* do you know that?"

"I had a lot of long, lonely nights to ponder very important things like that, as well as how giraffes mate, global warming, and the best wax for dripping on skin."

He chuckled. "That brain of yours never rests, and I like where it's headed. You can fulfill your dreams, too, Tabs. Move here, start your business. You can have it all."

"Carson, it's not that easy. You of all people know how hard it is to build a business. And mine would be such a niche. It will take a *lot* of hard work. Not that I'm afraid of it, but I do have to plan and prepare so I know what I'm in for. Besides, there's Adeline to consider."

He closed his eyes, soaking in her loving tone. "You really don't want to leave her, do you?"

"No," she whispered. "She was so shy when she first came to the orphanage, and scared of everyone and everything. I feel like I was supposed to meet her, and she's really come into her own. I don't know how long she'll be at the orphanage, but however long it is, I want to be there for her."

His heart broke for the little girl. He reached for Tawny's hand.

"I feel like half my heart is here with you," she said, "and half is there with her. I can't just abandon her. I don't want to."

"Then you shouldn't," he assured her. Too many women would toss money at less-fortunate children and feel they'd done their duty. Tawny would take every one of those children into her home and love, nurture, and protect them with her whole self. She was so real, so very *rare*, he'd never take that away. "But that doesn't mean you shouldn't consider opening your business. Even if in Paris." It killed him to say it, but how could he ask her to leave a child she clearly adored?

They both fell silent.

"I want you to have everything you've ever wanted," Carson finally said. "If Adeline owns a piece of you, then who am I to take that away from either of you? We'll figure the rest out, but don't put your hopes for a perfumery on hold." He had no idea *how* they'd figure it out, but they didn't have to do it that second. "You deserve to have your dreams come true."

"Like you?"

If only. "I fulfilled my career dreams, but I have yet to conquer the dreams that really matter."

She slid off his back, to his side, a sweet smile on her face. He turned to face her and gathered her against him, their naked bodies intertwining.

"What are your other dreams?" she asked as they each palmed the other's ass, keeping their bodies as close as could be.

"They're not what you think."

"Try me," she challenged.

"They have nothing to do with mating giraffes."

She laughed, and he pressed his lips to hers in a tender kiss, glad to set his worries aside for now.

"I had this friend once," he said. "She was a total bookworm, and into chemistry and computers and all things historic. I made her a promise when we first met that if she studied with me, one day I'd take her to the Speculum Alchemiae Museum. She was so excited to go to Prague and see the secret underground alchemy laboratory from the sixteenth century, she let me do dirty things to her for almost two whole years."

She gasped. "You *did* promise me that! But that's not why I let you do those things. I've been waiting a decade to go there. You sure take a long time to fulfill your promises."

He swept her beneath him, lacing their hands together beside her head. "Is that so?"

She bit her lower lip, trying to stifle an unstoppable giggle, and nodded.

He nipped at her lower lip, freeing it and kissing her. Her hips rose off the bed in an effort to align their bodies.

"Want something?" He pressed the head of his cock against

her slickness, rocking just hard enough to breach her entrance.

"I want *you*."

He lowered his mouth to hers as their bodies came together, and he loved her until they were both too tired to move. Then he held her close, and they fell back to sleep.

CARSON AWOKE HOURS later to the sun streaming through the curtains and Tawny snuggled soft and warm in his arms. He'd dreamed of waking with her in his arms, sharing days, and loving her through the nights, but nothing compared to her actually being there. How could he love someone so much that he didn't want to think about going a day without her? They kissed and laughed, and when they finally forced themselves from the bed, Carson carried Tawny's luggage into his bedroom and cleaned out a drawer.

"You can put your things in here, Tabs, and hang up anything you'd like in my closet."

"Thank you." She wrapped her arms around him, both of them still naked, and kissed his chest. "I didn't know what to expect when I showed up at the hotel and I don't feel like you minded, but I have to ask—"

He silenced her with a kiss, knowing his careful girl was suddenly worried he felt pushed into a corner. That was her cautious nature coming out, and he loved that she worried about him, but she needn't have.

"That's my answer, Tabs. You figure it out."

He went into the bathroom, brushed his teeth, and turned on the shower. When he came out, Tawny was standing by the balcony doors, holding her toiletries bag and looking like a gift from the heavens above.

"It's really beautiful here," she said. "The park reminds me of the campus. Does it remind you of it, too?"

He looked out at the snow-covered park and pressed a kiss to her shoulder. "Mm-hm. That's why I bought this house."

"I love knowing that." She touched his cheek. "You smell minty." Gazing outside, she said, "There must be eight inches out there."

"That's okay. We have no plans until later, when we go to Dylan's."

He led her into the steamy bathroom and stepped into the shower while she brushed her teeth. When she joined him under the warm shower spray, she brushed her slick body along his.

Her delicate fingers circled his cock. "The snowfall has nothing on you."

MAYBE IT WAS the number of years Tawny had gone without Carson, or maybe it was just that she loved him so much, making love with him was like discovering a new, exotic fragrance every single time. Whatever the reason, as she urged him to sit on the tiled bench in his very large shower, she wanted him more than she ever had.

She sank down to her knees, and he grabbed her arm, patting the bench beside him.

"Right here, baby. I want to be able to touch you, too."

She climbed onto all fours, lust coiling hot and tight inside her. He'd never been one to receive without wanting to give. He gathered her hair in one hand, watching as her fingers circled his cock, and she slicked her tongue over the head. He sucked in a long, slow breath, and the needy sound made her want to hear more. When she lowered her mouth over his cock, he tightened his grip on her hair, though he still let her control their speed as her hand followed her lips along the length of his shaft.

His other hand caressed her ass while the spray of the shower rained down on them. She loved him slowly, drawing out his pleasure, enjoying the way his muscles tensed with his effort not to take control. She drew back and slid her tongue around his swollen glans, holding his gaze.

"Suck," he said firmly.

She continued licking along his shaft, challenging him.

"*Suck*, Tabs."

The warning in his eyes made her insides clench. *Oh*, how she'd missed this! She continued teasing over and around his broad head, squeezing his shaft, but not stroking. The first crack of his hand on her ass brought tears of pleasure and a scintillating sting. He rubbed his palm over the tender spot, and she lowered her mouth over his cock. After all, he'd given her exactly what she'd wanted, and reciprocating gave her as much pleasure as receiving. She dragged her tongue along his shaft, his lower belly, his thighs, everywhere except where he needed it, earning another spank. By the third, her bottom was tender, and she moaned with the sting. He immediately tipped her face up, searching her eyes. The worry in his gaze made her heart so full of him she could barely think.

"Too much?"

"No," she managed, but she needed *him*.

She wanted to feel him lose control and to taste his essence. When she lowered her mouth again, he groaned. His hand moved between her legs. He pushed his fingers into her sex and his thumb into her ass, taking her right up to the brink of madness. She moaned around his cock.

"Christ, I love when you do that," he ground out between gritted teeth.

His hand in her hair helped guide their speed. He knew her so well, what she wanted *and* what she needed. He knew she was unable to concentrate on the incredible sensations he was doling out while pleasuring him. He guided her into a fast rhythm, matching the beat of his fingers and thumb, quickening the pace, breaching her harder, moving her mouth faster, until the world spun away and she shattered into a million pieces and his release pulsed warm and thick against the back of her throat as he grunted out her name.

When he gathered her in his arms and kissed her breathless, all those pieces of herself came back together.

Chapter Eight

CARSON'S TYPICAL SUNDAY routine included going for a run and then working for most of the day. Occasionally he'd join his brothers to watch a game, as he and Tawny were doing later that afternoon, but for the most part, weekdays and weekends blended together. Enjoying a leisurely day with Tawny had shown him what he'd been missing. Not the downtime—the *woman*. They binge-watched *The X-Files*, snacking on Junior Mints and popcorn, tossing them into each other's mouths until they tumbled over in fits of laughter. Tawny curled up beside him, just like old times, looking sexy and adorable in a pair of black leggings and an oversized white sweater that refused to stay on her shoulder. Carson took full advantage, tasting her shoulder as often as he liked and earning the sweet smiles he adored.

Now it was midafternoon, and they were taking a break from the television to go through the last two boxes from the storage unit.

Carson sat on the couch, and Tawny sat between his legs on the floor as he rubbed the tension from her shoulders.

"Eeny, meeny, miny, moe." She pointed to the boxes as she said the words.

He leaned down and kissed her cheek. "Tabs, it doesn't matter where the tiger hollers. You'll open the one you want to open first anyway."

She wrinkled her cute, upturned nose. "You're right." She patted one box. "This one is from college. It'll be easier." She pushed it away and tore the tape from the *other* box, the one marked with her mother's name, in her father's handwriting. She flatted her hand over the flaps and glanced at Carson with a nervous expression.

He moved to the floor beside her and draped an arm over her shoulder, bringing her closer. "You sure you're ready for this?"

"No, but I'm as ready as I'll ever be. Can I ask you something that you don't have to answer?"

"That's a loaded question. Sure."

"We didn't really talk about the fundraiser or your family, and I just realized that I kind of blew into your life and the most important thing about this weekend got pushed aside."

His mind spiraled back to a few weeks earlier, when he and his brothers had decided to honor Lorelei by making her the focus of the fundraiser and he'd gone to share the news with his mother. Overwhelmed with the freeing feeling of bringing memories of his baby sister into his life again, he'd fallen into his mother's arms like a giant child, and years of repressed emotions had come tumbling out. She'd said it was a feat of magic that it had finally happened. He'd argued that it was a coming together of the minds, a rational decision between brothers. His mother had shaken her head with a knowing smile and said, *I know you don't believe in magic, sweetheart, but Lorelei did. She's probably been sitting up in heaven wondering why her smart big brothers were taking so darn long to realize she's been with you all along. Sometimes all the rational thinking in the world won't get you what you need. It takes a little magic, and magic exists right here.* She'd patted his chest, over his heart.

"The fundraiser was important, but it wasn't the most important thing. You coming back to me on the night of the fundraiser? *That* is important. A sign even."

Her smiled warmed him. "You don't believe in signs."

"I never did." But he was starting to. Tawny was the only person he'd ever opened up to about Lorelei. Wasn't that a sign of how deeply he'd trusted her? The fact that she'd reappeared in his life on the night they'd chosen to celebrate Lorelei's life after all these years had to mean something.

A shy expression came over her. "Me, either. But can anything be more of a sign than what my father said to me?"

"Some would argue that he was the catalyst for change. And the sign was the sold-out hotel."

She rolled her eyes. "This is why we don't do signs. Because everything can be interpreted differently. I wanted to ask about your family. When you first told me about your sister, you said your parents had split up after she'd passed away and that your father had turned angry and bitter. I've always wondered if things had gotten better for your family."

Carson sat up a little straighter, putting a few inches between him and Tawny, a typical reaction when someone mentioned his father, which wasn't often. At six foot four, Gerard Bad had a commanding presence, and he used it to his advantage in the courtroom. He was a leading criminal attorney, as manipulative and devious as they came. Before Lorelei had gotten sick, their father had been a typical overworked attorney, but he'd been a good father. After they'd lost Lorelei, he'd turned hateful toward everyone, most of all his family. Two years later their father was still storming through the house, raging at every little thing and arguing with everyone. Carson's oldest brother, Mick, had stood up to their father and finally gotten him to do what he'd already mentally done. *Leave* his family for good.

"We don't have to talk about him." Tawny reached for his hand.

She had such a big heart. She should be worried about herself, gearing up for what he was sure would be an emotional ride when she saw her parents' belongings, but instead she was thinking about him.

"It's okay. Mick got married a few months ago, to Amanda. She's terrific. You'll meet her later at Dylan's. My father attended their wedding, and he was less angry, but still bitter. He'd never shown up for the fundraisers in the past, and we didn't expect him to be there this year, especially since this was the first time we'd honored Lorelei with posters, as you might have seen at the hotel. For us, honoring her was a really good thing."

"I remember you mentioning that your family hadn't really talked about her."

Carson was eleven when Lorelei died, and he'd retreated from life, holing up in his room to deal with the devastation of losing the sister he adored. Lorelei had been a shining star in their house. As the youngest of five, she had a zest for life that put them to shame. She was inquisitive as hell, and inserted herself into her older brothers' lives every way she could. She'd shared Carson's love of science fiction and insisted on watching all the scary movies with him. By the end of them she'd be curled up beside him peeking out from a quarter-sized hole in a blanket. She claimed it made the shows less scary. After she died, the house had felt colder, their lives had felt emptier, and Carson hadn't been able to put words to the emptiness he'd felt.

With his father's bitterness, he wouldn't have risked it anyway. In his despair, he buried his thoughts in trying to understand why Lorelei had died so quickly. That was the year Carson learned to hack computers. He'd needed answers, and he'd hacked into the hospital database to find them. He'd quickly learned that tests and medical conclusions weren't answers that could help him with his pain. He'd disappeared from the world for months on end, save for attending school, but Mick had finally dragged his ass out into the world again and helped him find his footing.

"We didn't," Carson finally responded. "I talked to you about Lorelei, but no one else. It was too hard, and talking about her was a trigger for my father's anger. We learned to keep our mouths shut. But Dylan's new girlfriend, Tiffany, convinced him it was time to reopen the doors we'd closed and honor her. As hard as it was to see Lorelei's pictures on the posters, we all desperately needed it. Anyway, our father showed up at the event. I didn't see him. He was only there a few minutes. But Dylan said he'd told him he did a good job by honoring Lorelei. I think he's softening around the edges. Talk about regrets. That's a man whose bed is made of them."

"I hope you can mend that fence at some point. At least you and your brothers are talking about your sister again. That's good, right?" She tucked her hair behind her ear. "And your mom? Is she doing okay?"

"She's doing great." He knew she was fishing now, buying time before going through her parents' things. "How is *Tawny?*"

"Nervous, but good." Her eyes shifted to the box. "What do you think he saved from my mom?"

"There's only one way to find out."

"Thank you for being here with me," she said as she lifted

the flaps.

"It's my house," he teased, trying to lighten the mood.

She gave him a saucy look, then peered into the box. "Oh my gosh." She withdrew a handful of crayon drawings on the type of oversized paper kids used when they were learning to write with dashed and solid lines on the bottom and space at the top for pictures. An expression of happiness and longing washed over her. "I can't believe he kept my drawings."

Carson took in the crayon drawings of people, a house, and things he couldn't discern, and he read the words scrawled on the bottom. "My family. Tawny Faith Bishop." He pressed a kiss to her temple. "I still think you have the most beautiful name I've ever heard."

"Thank you. I always felt like having my mom's name as my middle name made her an even bigger part of me."

"I know. I remember you telling me that."

She looked at the drawings with a small smile. "I used to confuse my teachers, because I told them my mom lived with us until I was in the second grade. They must have thought I was crazy since she died the year before. But at home? She was everywhere. My father didn't empty out her closet for the longest time. I was always getting into her things. Wearing her scarves, traipsing around in her high heels. I don't know how he stood it."

"I do," Carson said softly. "Seeing glimpses of his wife in his daughter must have made it easier. I would have done anything to have those kinds of reminders of Lorelei after we lost her, instead of the darkness we all fell into."

She rested her head on his shoulder. "I'm sorry it was so hard for you and your family. Why don't you have any family photos anywhere?"

He pulled his wallet from his pocket and opened it, showing her the picture of his family he'd carried for as long as he could remember. He was sitting cross-legged on the grass, shoulder to shoulder with his brothers. Behind them, their parents stood arm in arm. Lorelei was perched on their father's hip, beaming at the camera.

"You still carry it?" She looked at the picture, running her finger over the ragged edges. "Even though I saw this in college, I still can't get over how different you looked. You were all elbows and knees, and that hair? It's so long." She touched his cheek. "You still had the soft cheeks of a boy. You were all really cute. You were eight in this, right?"

"Yeah."

"But this doesn't tell me why you don't have other pictures. I have pictures of my mom and dad all over my place."

"Why do you ask the questions no one else ever has?" He put the picture away, trying to figure out how to admit the truth. Talking with Tawny had always helped ease the emptiness his little sister left behind, but she had a knack for getting to the heart of things.

"Because I see you in a way no one else ever has. If you're still the same way you were in college, then to your friends, you're a quiet, private guy. It wouldn't seem odd for you not to have pictures. But the Carson I know would think he was protecting his family in some way. But why? That's what I want to know." She gazed into his eyes as if she were looking for the answers. "Or am I way off base? Lord knows it's been a long time. You could have changed a lot."

A laugh fell from his lips. "You're gifted, Tabs. In a sense you're right. I'm protecting someone, but it's not them. My family includes Lorelei, and it always will. I had pictures of her up when I first moved in, but it stopped my family cold, so I took them down. But now that we've all started opening doors to our past, maybe it's time to put them back up."

He pushed to his feet and went to a chest in the corner of the room, retrieving a few framed family photos. His pulse kicked up at the sight of his family as a unit, inclusive of both Lorelei and their father. His sister had long brown hair and big, inquisitive eyes, too wise for her age. His father wore an actual smile, and Carson's throat thickened at having lost not just his sister, but his father. He was thankful the rest of them remained close, though they'd all changed. He and his brothers were harder, more closed off, and his mother poured her heart into nurturing plants, as if they were her children.

He set the frames on the mantel, and Tawny pushed to her feet.

She looked thoughtfully at the photos. "These are all from when you were kids."

"That's all I've got that have my whole family. Lorelei died when I was eleven," he reminded her. He reached up to the top shelf and retrieved a frame that had been facedown. "Maybe I can put this one up again, too."

He handed her the picture of the two of them hugging. Her hand moved over her gaping mouth. "Where did this come from? Who took it?"

"Brett took it on his phone when he came up with my parents our junior year, and I had it printed. I think you were leaving to see your dad, and you came by to pick up a book—"

"Notes. I came by to pick up my notes. I remember now." She blinked up at him with a tenuous smile. "When did you turn it over?"

"It never made it to the mantel in this house. I just couldn't stand to put it away for good. In my other house, I turned it over right after I tracked you down, a couple years after you were married. I'd just started my business, and I was in Chicago meeting with one of Mick's clients who was considering using our firm. I just had to see you with my own eyes, to see that you were happy. You weren't on social media, so I looked up Keith. I have no idea what I was thinking. I went by your house and saw you two kissing in the driveway, and I knew I'd crossed a line. Some part of me had hoped you might be divorced, but…I'm sorry, Tawny. I shouldn't have breached your privacy that way, and I never did it again."

"It's okay. I get it, Carson. I showed up at your family's fundraiser uninvited and unannounced. There's really no difference. I think the universe was telling us something."

She wiped the dust from the picture and set it on the mantel. "I think you should definitely put this back up. Things between us are moving so fast, it's a nice reminder that we aren't a new couple. We have more history than most people could ever dream of."

THEY SETTLED IN on the floor again, and Tawny began going through the box. They looked at a photo album from when she was a little girl, and she couldn't believe how much she'd looked like her mother, even then. They found a few of her father's work journals and Tawny's sixth-grade science notebook. Even then she'd been meticulous about note taking.

"I remember trying to get out of doing homework so I could go read," Tawny said as she put the notebook down beside her. "I told my father that my brain could only hold so much information in one night and that I wanted it to have room for whatever book I was reading."

Carson smiled. "How'd that go over?"

"He heated up a pot of water and handed me a cup of sugar. The water represented my brain, the sugar was knowledge. He told me to pour in the sugar, and we stood at the stove as I poured and he stirred. Sure enough, the sugar dissolved, which he likened to the brain's endless capacity to absorb knowledge. But he took it further, because that was my dad, always teaching. We did the same experiment with cold water, and of course the sugar dissolved slower and hit a saturation point. My father said if I didn't continue feeding my brain, it wouldn't react as efficiently." She smiled with the memory. "I never tried to outsmart him again."

Carson leaned over and kissed her. "You did better. You decided to be *smarter* than him."

"You remember that story, huh?" She'd forgotten she'd already shared it with him. She'd read *after* finishing her homework that night, but not the fiction novel she'd intended to read. Instead, she'd gone online and researched saturation points, absorption rates, and everything she could find about the brain's capacity to learn. That night had sparked her love of all things chemistry related.

"You're pretty unforgettable, Tabs. Remember when I used to tell you that there was more to life than good grades and you needed to save room in your head for fun?"

"That was the pot calling the kettle black, Mr. I Won't Settle for Less Than a 4.0 Average."

He barreled in to her, tickling her ribs and making her squeal with delight.

"Kettle?" he said. "You were right there with me, competing

for the highest grades, and you know it."

"So?" She laughed. "Remember what I said when you made those comments?"

"Let's get the sugar," they said in unison, and he lowered his mouth to hers.

She pushed playfully at his chest. "We'll be late for Dylan's if we start messing around."

"Who needs football?" He waggled his brows as he sat up. "I get a kiss for every touchdown."

"From which team?" She didn't even know who was playing, but she didn't care. She'd never watched a whole football game, and she was looking forward to getting to know the brothers who meant so much to Carson.

"Both teams." He peeked at his phone. "We'd better get a move on so we're not late. Let's finish going through your dad's stuff."

"If you'd stop kissing me," she teased, withdrawing a shoe box from among her father's things. Inside were dozens of letters addressed to her father, dated from before she was born until a month before her mother was killed.

She sat back against the couch with the open shoe box on her lap, her heart banging out a troubled beat inside her. "They're from my mother. These letters could tell me more about her."

Carson's arm circled her shoulder, and he kissed her temple, remaining silent. That was his way, giving her time and space to get her thoughts out.

"My father said she'd written love letters to him, remember? These are private. I shouldn't read them." She met Carson's thoughtful gaze. "Why would he have left them for me when he could have gotten rid of them?"

"Maybe he didn't want your mother's memory to die with him," he suggested. "Or maybe there's something in the letters he wanted you to discover for yourself. To see your mother through her writing, instead of through his interpretation of her."

Her pulse went crazy as she lifted out a letter and peeked into the envelope.

"A picture," she said, taking it out. It was a photograph of her parents in front of Biology, the café where they'd met in New York City. "Look at their big eighties hair, and those clothes!"

"Your mom was beautiful, Tabs. It's like looking at you," Carson said. "You have her hair, her almond eyes, even her pretty nose." He kissed the tip of her nose. "I love your nose."

She smiled, warmed by his sweetness. "That's good, because it's the only one I have. I wonder when this picture was taken. They met in seventy-eight, when they were attending separate graduate schools. I told you this story, right?"

"You did. Your mom was in the city with friends when they met, and every year after that, they had lunch at that café on the anniversary of the day they'd met. They got married on that same day, three years later. And after you lost your mom, you and your father carried on the tradition at the café."

"I love that you remember."

"It's part of you. I'll never forget."

He leaned in for a kiss—he was always leaning in for kisses now, which was new and wonderful, and she knew she'd never tire of it.

"Now it'll be me and you having lunch at the café. We won't let that tradition die," he promised.

"I'd really like that." She gazed at the picture of her parents, trying to suppress a wave of sadness and wishing not only that she'd had more time with her mother, but also that her mother could have met Carson. She hoped her father was watching over her and knew that she was finding her own skin again—chasing happiness instead of trying to become someone she wasn't.

"I wish I had known my mother better so I could remember more about her," she admitted. "I'm thankful that through my father's stories, she always felt like she was present in our lives. I think some people might find that creepy, but my father adored her until the day he died." She pressed the photo to her chest. "Do you think it's weird that I grew up with a father who showed me what true love was, even in my mother's absence, and I ran off and married someone I wasn't really in love with just to escape feeling out of control?"

"Not at all," Carson said, pulling her in closer. "Your father taught you how to love endlessly, the way he loved you and your mother. Fear might have driven you in a different direction, but your heart never forgot. You came back, Tabs, and if I have my way, we'll never be apart again."

Chapter Nine

TAWNY DECIDED NOT to read the letters yet, and to take some time to think about them. They didn't have time to finish going through the boxes before leaving for Dylan's, but she was no longer afraid to do so. She knew she could get through anything with Carson there to support her. If she cried, he'd hold her. If she laughed, he'd laugh with her. And if she just needed a moment—*or a day*—of introspection, he'd give her that, too. She wished she'd clung to that belief in college, instead of running scared.

When Barton arrived to drive them to Dylan's, he stepped inside, bringing his woody, leathery scent with him. He handed Carson a big package wrapped in gold paper. With a friendly smile and a professional nod, he went to the curb and waited by the car.

Carson's lips tipped up as he handed the gift to Tawny. "For you, my beautiful girl."

"Carson...?"

He winked, and her stomach fluttered. "Open it, baby."

"What have you done?" she mumbled to herself. The wrapping was so pretty, she didn't want to tear it. She carefully lifted the tape from the edges and slid the box from the paper.

He took the wrapping from her hands and lifted the lid, revealing a stunning pair of black leather knee-high boots with

Burberry's signature beige, brown, and red–check trim around the calf and a gorgeous gold buckle. They matched her outfit and her camel-colored coat perfectly.

"I can't let my girl go around the Big Apple with ankle boots when there's eight inches of snow on the ground."

"Carson, I can't accept these. They cost more than my airfare to get here, and how do you even know what size I wear?"

He wrapped his arms around her, grinning down at her. "You're welcome."

He pressed his lips to hers, obviously pleased with himself for skipping right over her question.

One blissful kiss and she melted against him. "This was sweet of you, but you don't have to buy me things."

He led her to the couch and knelt before her, taking off her ankle boots and helping her on with the new ones. The soft leather felt heavenly.

"Perfect fit."

"Thank you, but really, you don't have to—"

He silenced her with a glare, boxing her in with one hand on either side of her. His biceps strained against the sleeves of his dark T-shirt as he leaned in until his lips nearly touched hers. "What I do for you will never be driven by what's expected of me, so please don't say that again, okay? I want to give you the world, but I won't, since you seem to have a thing about receiving gifts. I'm starting slow, getting you used to the idea." He kissed her softly. "And one day." He kissed her jaw. "You'll stop wondering why." He kissed her neck, making her breathe harder. "Because you'll know." He pulled the collar of her sweater down and kissed her breastbone. Then he gazed into her eyes again and said, "That everything I do for you is done out of love."

At a loss for words, she wound her hands around his neck and kissed him. His chest came down over her and his arms circled her body, holding her so tight she could barely breathe.

"Thank you," she said as they drew apart. "They're elegant, and beautiful, and almost as divine as you."

He chuckled and gave her a chaste kiss. "Come on, Tabs. I'm looking forward to introducing you to my family and seeing if you're still worried other people will find out about all those dirty things we do together."

"You haven't even started doing dirty things to me yet," she said with a smirk.

"Soon, baby," he said cockily.

Her nerves rattled to life again. "Hold on. Do your brothers *know* what we used to do?"

"I told you I would never share what we did with anyone," he said in his most serious voice. "Especially my brothers. Brett has no filter. God only knows what would pop out of his mouth at the wrong time." His hand circled her waist as they headed to the coat closet. "Do you think I want them visualizing you in the positions I'm going to get you in later?"

Oh my. "How am I supposed to make it through the evening with *that* in my head?" She stopped walking and tugged him down by his shirt so she could look into his eyes. "Do *not* get me hot and bothered before we get there, or I *will* worry about it." She softened her tone at the amusement in his eyes. "And thank you again for the boots. I love them. It was thoughtful of you to buy them for me. I'm just not used to people buying me things, but they're gorgeous, and they feel like they were made for my feet."

"Kind of like how my cock is made for your—"

"Carson!" She swatted him, loving his playful side as much

as she loved his naughty side.

"Oh," he said, feigning wide-eyed innocence. "You meant no dirty talk, either?" He grabbed her ass. "I thought you only meant I should refrain from *touching* you in a sexual way."

He chuckled and helped her on with her coat.

"Don't tease me. This feels like finals week, where I know in my head that I understand the material, but the wrong answer could obliterate all my hard work."

He tugged her against him and framed her face with his hands. "Tabs, take a deep breath."

She did, and she focused on his serious expression rather than her racing heart.

"Listen to me. You've spent years trying to outrun us, and you couldn't do it any more than I could. No matter what anyone says tonight—and my brothers will probably make sexual comments and innuendos, because they're guys and that's what they do—they're only *fishing*, okay? Mick knows I fell hard for you in college, because he helped me pick up the pieces after you married Keith, but that's where it ended. Nobody knows what we did, what we do, or what we might do in the future except you and me." He brushed his thumb over her jaw. "I promise you, if something inappropriate is said, I will intervene. I will protect your privacy, and our intimacy, with everything I have. Okay?"

"Yes." She swallowed the unexpected sadness bubbling up inside her.

"What is it? Did I make you even more anxious?"

She shook her head. "No. I wish I had told you how I felt all those years ago. And I'm so sorry I hurt you."

"Don't worry, beautiful. I plan on making up for lost time, and then some." He swatted her ass. "Let's go. If we're too late they'll think we were having sex."

Her eyes widened and he laughed.

"I was kidding, but we could"—he looked toward the stairs—"beat them to the punch."

She dragged him out the door by his sleeve. "Down, boy."

"Hm, I see a little role-playing in our future."

AS THEY WAITED for the elevator in Dylan's building, Tawny's nerves flared. She tucked her hair behind her ear, smoothed her coat over her sweater, fidgeted with her earring.

Carson reached for her hand. "Still nervous?"

The elevator arrived and they stepped inside. She held up her finger and thumb, indicating *a little* as he pressed the button for Dylan's floor.

As soon as the doors closed, his mouth came down over hers. He trapped her against the wall, pinning her hands above her head as he deepened the kiss. He was deliciously hard all over, rubbing his body against hers. She felt every swipe of his tongue all over her body, and her worries drifted away.

"I've got you, babe. I've always got you," he said into her ear seconds before sinking his teeth into her neck.

"Oh *God. Carson*—"

He kissed the tender spot on her neck and lowered her hands, kissing each of her wrists. "Don't ever be ashamed of what you feel, baby."

"I asked you not to get me hot and bothered," she said breathlessly, trying to regain control of her runaway desires. But when she looked up at him, all she saw was his mouth, and she wanted more steamy kisses. "Now I'm going to be thinking about making out with you, and they'll be able to tell."

He tipped her chin up, his eyes as serious as the day was long. "It's normal to want your partner, in public or in private. You were going to worry anyway, Tabs. We both know that. I would rather you had something *real* to think about than worry for the sake of worrying. I'm going to prove to you that what you feel is normal if it's the last thing I do."

"I know it's normal to think about you. But it became too consuming before." She pressed her hands to her chest. "My heart is beating so fast."

"Isn't it better to be thinking about kissing me than worrying what anyone else thinks?" The elevator doors opened and they stepped into the hall. Carson didn't head for Dylan's apartment. He stood outside the elevator holding her hand and gazing into her eyes.

Making sure I'm okay.

"It is better," she admitted.

"Good, because they're going to think you want me no matter what. I've never introduced them to a girlfriend." When she opened her mouth to argue that point, he cut her off. "I don't date, remember?"

She blew out a breath. "No pressure there. The *only* girl they've met? Geez! We should have had you bringing a string of women around so they'd be used to it."

"Don't even…"

She smiled with his warning. He was so loyal, so careful, so…*mine.*

"Are you ready to think rationally?" he asked.

"Almost," she said with a laugh.

"Good, because I need your analytical brain to hear this. You didn't react like that when we were out yesterday around strangers, which makes me think that what sets you into panic mode is feeling out of control around people who know us."

She narrowed her eyes, realizing what he'd done. "You were testing me. Doing research! You totally kissed me in the elevator to see how I'd react."

"'A detective with his murder mystery, a chemist seeking the structure of a new compound, use little of the formal and logical modes of reasoning. Through a series of intuitions, surmises, fancies, they stumble upon the right explanation, and have a knack of seizing it when it once comes within reach,'" Carson said.

He was quoting Gilbert Lewis, a chemist whose contributions to valence bond theory shaped modern theories of chemical bonding. She loved that he knew she'd get that reference. God, she'd missed this back-and-forth and his intimate knowledge of what made her tick.

"I cannot believe you seized your moment in the elevator. You're..." She glanced down the hall, searching for the right words. "You're the only person in the world who gets me, Carson. I should be mad at you, but how can I be? You're totally, frustratingly *right*. Why have I never put those things together before? How could I have missed something so rudimentary?"

"Sometimes we're too caught up in the outcome to see how we got there," he said thoughtfully.

"*If* your theory is true, how do we fix it? What if I panic around your brothers like I did in college?"

"You won't."

"How can you be so sure?" she protested, wanting assurances she knew he couldn't provide.

"Because this time you're not trying to handle any of your

feelings alone." He pulled her closer, his embrace calming her erratic pulse. "We've got this, Tabs. Trust me."

She was wrong.

He was the *only* person who could provide the assurance she needed.

WHEN CARSON WAS in college, he'd fantasized about spending time with Tawny and his brothers. He'd put those thoughts away long ago, but watching his brothers fall in love, and spending time with them and their significant others, had brought back all the *what-ifs*. Now, as they stood outside Dylan's door, he hoped like hell his brothers would keep their comments tame.

When Brett answered Dylan's door, the look on his face told Carson that hoping wasn't going to get him very far. He held Tawny a little tighter.

"Bro!" Brett said overenthusiastically. Like all the Bad brothers, he was a couple inches over six feet tall, with dark hair and dark eyes—that were currently sliding down the length of Tawny's body.

Carson grabbed Brett, an ex-cop who outweighed him by about twenty pounds of muscle, and hauled him into a manly embrace, speaking sternly, and quietly, into his ear. "Look at her like that again and I *will* kill you." He released him with a shove, sending Brett stumbling back.

"Whoa, dude. I was just admiring how exquisitely Tawny had grown up." Brett schooled his expression and lowered his chin, looking at Tawny with a friendly—instead of lustful—grin. "Tawny Bishop. You've grown up to be a gorgeous woman. What are you doing with this guy?"

Carson rolled his eyes as Brett embraced her. Tawny laughed, *thank God*.

"Hi, Brett," she said. "Other than that scruff on your chin, you haven't changed one bit since you were a kid."

Brett lifted his arms and flexed his biceps, which Carson had to admit were bigger than life. *The bastard*. He had a body like Henry Cavill in *Superman*, but he hadn't gotten those muscles driven by a need to be strong. Brett was like a stick of dynamite, full of anger that had developed after they'd lost Lorelei. It had clung to him like a second skin. He worked out to work *off* his demons.

Brett winked at Tawny. "I beg to differ, sweetheart. I'm bigger, smarter, and when you get tired of Carson, I'll show you that I'm manlier, too."

"Watch it, little brother," Carson warned.

Tawny slid an arm around Carson's waist and said, "Guess you didn't get the memo. Real men don't have to prove it."

Holy hell. She pulled that off like she was made of steel. The only hint Carson had that she was nervous was the soft laugh that bubbled out afterward. Damn, he loved her.

"Whoa!" Tiffany peered around Brett, her blond hair tumbling over her shoulders. "Someone got told off with class."

Brett chuckled. "All kidding aside, it's really good to see you again, Tawny. I'm glad you're here." He eyed Carson. "And by the look on my brother's face—"

"Brett," Carson warned.

"What?" Brett took a step back as they walked inside and closed the door. "I was going to say that you were glad, too."

"Okay," Tiffany said, pulling Brett out of the way. She and Amanda, Mick's wife, sidled up to Tawny with welcoming smiles. "That's enough *Brett* for now. Ignore him. I'm Tiffany, Dylan's girlfriend, and this is Amanda, Mick's wife, and we're really glad you're here."

"Thanks," Tawny said. "It's nice to meet you both."

"Don't worry. You'll get used to Brett," Amanda assured her. "He comes on strong, but he's just marking his territory. Now that he's puffed his tail feathers, he'll calm down. Here." She reached for Tawny's coat. "Let me take that."

"Thank you."

As Tawny shrugged off her coat, Carson embraced Tiffany, who whispered, "She is stunning! Where have you been hiding her?"

In my heart. "Tawny and I went to college together," he explained, and bent to hug Amanda. "Where are Dylan and Mick?"

"I'm right here," Dylan said as he came down the hallway.

"My hubby got called out of town for a meeting," Amanda said. "One of his celebrity clients got herself into a sticky situation. He said he was going to call you once he figured out when he'd be back in town so he could meet Tawny."

"Great. If you need anything while he's gone, let me know," Carson offered.

"Brett and I've got her covered, too." Dylan patted him on the back. "Good to see you, bro."

"You have all these overprotective guys to look forward to," Amanda said to Tawny. "Having grown up with only one sister, it's wonderful the way these guys just scoop you up and make you part of the family."

"I can only imagine." Tawny looked adoringly at Carson.

Dylan turned a charming smile on her. "Ah, the elusive Tawny Bishop. I thought Carson had made you up back in college. It's nice to meet you." He embraced her, quick and friendly. Then he settled a hand on Tiffany's back and nuzzled her neck. "I see you met my beautiful Summers."

"Hello?" Amanda said, heading for the kitchen. "I'm without my man tonight, remember? Maybe you should take that into the bedroom."

"Come on, Tawny, let's get you a drink." Tiffany looped her arm in Tawny's, dragging her away from Carson.

He held on to her fingers as long as he could.

"I'll bring her back," Tiffany promised.

Tawny glanced over her shoulder and he mouthed, *Are you okay?*

She smiled and nodded.

"Dude, you've been stripped of your woman." Dylan headed for the living room, where Brett was watching the pre-game show. "Take your coat off and chill."

Carson put his coat over the back of a chair. He heard the girls giggling and sank down to the couch beside Dylan, watching Tawny. If she was nervous, he couldn't tell.

"Relax," Dylan said in a hushed voice. "She's in good hands. So, what's the deal?"

"The deal is, he's finally getting laid," Brett said.

"Do me a favor," Carson said to Brett. "Watch the sex talk around Tabs, okay?"

Brett and Dylan exchanged a curious look.

"Tabs?" Brett arched a brow.

Christ, how could he have forgotten that Brett would ask about every little thing? He ground his teeth together and squared his shoulders. Brett might have him in size, but Carson had him in speed, and Brett knew it. Carson wasn't a fighter, but he had no patience for bullshit where Tawny was concerned. "A nickname from school. *Don't push*, Brett. I'm not messing around, okay? Tawny's important to me, and if you fuck this up, I'll fuck *you* up."

Brett held up his hands in surrender. "Hey, I want you to be happy. I was kidding. I'll tone it down as best I can." He glanced in the kitchen, where the girls were leaning head to head, talking and laughing. "Just tell me one thing. Were you two a *thing* in college?"

The question caught Dylan's attention. Carson weighed his answer carefully. He didn't want to give Brett any fuel for his fire, but he also wanted them to know exactly how important she was to him.

"We've always been a thing," he finally answered. "But not the type of *thing* you think, so respect her. Got it?"

Chapter Ten

TAWNY HAD NEVER understood society's fascination with sports, but watching the football game with everyone was actually *fun*. Not that Tawny knew more than the basics—each team's goal was to make a touchdown. And she was in awe of Tiffany, who was a sports agent and was as vehement about her favorite players, some of whom were her clients, as the guys were. Just listening to them give each other a hard time showed her an aggressive side of Carson she had never seen. His brothers seemed to know how to push his buttons. She liked seeing that side of him. She'd always known it was there, but Carson didn't need to prove himself the way other men did. He was secure in his manhood.

As well you should be. Mm-hm. I do love your manhood.

At halftime, Amanda leaned closer to Tawny, eyeing Tiffany. "Isn't she amazing? She knows everything about sports. I can barely keep the teams straight. I just like to be around everyone." She and Tiffany were so easy to get along with, it had taken only a few minutes for Tawny to get past her initial nervousness.

"I'm with you," Tawny admitted. "All I know is, when Carson cheers, I cheer."

"That's my girl." Carson rubbed his nose along her cheek and whispered, "Are you doing okay? We can leave at any time."

She loved that he was willing to turn his world upside down for her, but she didn't need, or want, him to. He sat beside her with one hand resting on her leg, pulling her in for kisses after touchdowns and during commercials. She'd only flinched the first time or two, as the others had teased them about getting a room, which somehow made her feel *more* comfortable. It was a wonderful feeling trying to understand her fears and conquer them *with* him.

"I'm more than okay. Thanks."

He moved in for another kiss.

"Dude." Brett splayed his hands. "I've got no woman here. Do you mind not lip-locking every three seconds?"

"Yeah, I do," Carson said, and kissed Tawny again.

"You could call Sophie," Amanda suggested. "She likes football."

Brett's brows lifted. "Duly noted."

"Who's Sophie?" Tawny asked.

"She's Mick's assistant, and she's *gorgeous*." Amanda looked at Brett and said, "Every client who comes through our door practically drools when they meet her. I'm surprised she's not already off the market."

"Brett's had a thing for Sophie for years," Carson said. "But he's too chicken to ask her out."

Brett scoffed. "Chicken my ass. It's all about timing."

Amanda laughed. "Timing? More like finding the right line. You've made innuendos about tying her up and sleeping with her. She's too classy for that."

Tawny's ears buzzed as she processed Amanda's comment. *Brett offered to tie Sophie up?* She stole a glance at Carson, whose brows knitted, and just as quickly she saw understanding dawning on him.

He hugged her and whispered, "He has no idea about us."

She breathed a little easier, but she stole a glance at Brett and Dylan, wondering if all of Carson's brothers were into various sexual games.

"I mean, maybe she'd like being tied up," Amanda added. "But not until she's treated properly and *trusts* you."

"Trust is *everything*," Tiffany added.

As Tawny listened to the girls, her pulse quickened. In college she'd had no frame of reference, no girlfriends she was comfortable discussing sex with. If she had, she might have learned that what she and Carson did together was not that far out of the norm. She wasn't even sure anymore that it was what they'd done that had freaked her out as much as that keeping it a secret had turned it into something taboo in her mind.

"I'm priming her." Brett smirked. "I'm not the kind of guy who wines and dines women. I need to do things on my own timeline. Sex, *then* dinner. Wait, no. Sex, more sex, *then* real food to power up for round three."

"No wonder you don't have a girlfriend. Not that I'm judging or anything. I had no time for boyfriends before Dylan refused to go unnoticed," Tiffany said with a loving gaze locked on her man. "Hey, maybe Dylan can give you pointers on how to be romantic."

"He's romantic because he's got *girly* genes," Brett teased. "So in touch with his feelings he has to talk them out all the time."

Dylan pulled Tiffany onto his lap. "Jealous? Look what my girly genes got me."

"Okay, enough bumping chests, you apes. Poor Tawny is going to think you guys do nothing but tease each other."

Tiffany climbed off his lap, and the three men chuckled.

"I want to hear about Paris," Tiffany said, inserting herself between Carson and Tawny on the couch.

"Tiff…?" Carson shook his head as he made space for her.

"It's halftime." Tiffany wiggled her behind, forcing him to give her more room. "It's the only time I can talk without missing the game. Tawny, I want to know everything. Is it as fabulous as everyone says? Do you have family there?"

"It's just me," Tawny said. "I don't have any siblings. My mother died when I was young, and my father passed away two years ago. I moved to Paris right after I lost him."

Carson's expression softened, and he stretched an arm behind Tiffany and laid his hand on Tawny's shoulder. A healing touch. She covered his hand with hers, their eyes connecting, and her heart squeezed.

"Oh gosh, I'm so sorry," Amanda said.

"Me too," Tiffany said. "Everyone needs family, so consider yourself part of ours, right, Amanda?"

"Absolutely," Amanda agreed. "Sisters from another mother. We'll have to exchange phone numbers." She pulled her phone from her pocket, and Tiffany grabbed hers from the coffee table. "What's your number?"

Tawny was stunned by how readily they welcomed her into their inner circle. She gave them her phone number, and they each texted her. She'd left her phone at Carson's house, but she was excited to know she'd have their numbers. She'd been so busy since moving to Paris that she didn't have many friends there, and the ones she had were more like acquaintances.

"Welcome to the tribe," Dylan said.

Tribe. She wanted to be part of the tribe. She'd been alone for far too long. Emotions bubbled up inside her, and she glanced at Carson, whose expression was as full of happiness as she felt.

"The Bad Boys Girl Tribe," Amanda said with a laugh. "Now, tell us all about what you do in *Grand Paris*." She said the last two words with an accent.

"I'm a perfumer." She glanced at Carson and added, "I can't believe I'm actually saying this, but I'm considering starting my own boutique perfumery. Something very different from what's currently available."

The surprise, and overriding approval, in Carson's eyes encouraged her.

"Wow." Amanda tucked her dark hair behind her ear. "I've never met a perfumer. You actually *make* perfumes? How cool is that?"

Tawny tapped her nose. "I've always been able to identify scents, and I've always devoured everything I could about science the way women go through romance novels."

"Romance novels?" Amanda raised her hand. "I'm a Jill Shalvis junkie!"

"That's how I am about what I do. I love my job, but I will say that being able to smell every little thing isn't always as lovely as it sounds."

"Like Brett after he eats chili," Dylan said.

Brett kicked his foot.

"Tawny, what will be different about your shop?" Tiffany asked.

"I want to create personalized fragrances instead of mass-market perfumes for retailers."

"You mean, like you meet people and develop a perfume just for them?" Amanda asked.

"Yes, exactly," Tawny said.

"How can you do that?" Amanda asked. "I mean, how do you know what a person's perfume should smell like?"

Tawny shrugged. "I'm not sure how to explain it, because I think some of what I do is an inherent skill. My father taught me to separate sensory input when I was a little girl, and I've gotten really good at it. I can tell you exactly what fragrances you should be wearing."

"Really?" Amanda squealed. "Tell me! Mick would *so* love this. We'll be your first customers! Oh, if you make one for me, can you call it *Freckles*? Please?" Her cheeks flushed, and she said, "It's a private thing between me and Mick."

That piqued Tawny's curiosity. *Where exactly are those freckles?* Pushing her nosiness aside, she focused on envisioning a scent for Amanda, which would now include this hidden side of her. This was where Tawny shined, pairing off people with fragrances that could bring out sides of them they may not even know existed.

"Sure," she said. "You're very feminine, and your strength is evident in the way you carry yourself and insert yourself into situations. I'd play off that, giving you a base note of red rose and vanilla to captivate and reel Mick in. The base notes become more noticeable later in the day, after the top and medium notes have worn off. I see you as *intimate*, with a hidden adventurous side. I think chamomile and geranium would speak to your femininity, with a touch of lemongrass and tangerine, to play off of your bright personality. But you need something richer, like the dry heat of Oriental amber."

"Dry heat sounds so sensual," Amanda said. "I think I'd like that."

They were all watching Tawny, listening intently, but it was the way Carson was watching her, as if he were falling in love with her right there and then, in front of everyone, that made her heart race. She tried to concentrate on what she was saying and not how badly she wanted to continue gazing into his eyes.

"That's a starting point," Tawny explained. "Fragrances smell different on everyone, and some fragrances need to be tweaked hundreds of times before they're perfect."

"Do me!" Tiffany said.

"Hey." Dylan hauled Tiffany onto his lap again. "You're only allowed to be *done* by me."

"You are so possessive!" Tiffany kissed him. "Tawny, do me, please?"

Carson moved closer, and his arm circled Tawny's shoulder. He began moving his fingers along the base of her neck in a dizzying pattern. His gaze was so intense, she wanted to talk about fragrances twenty-four seven just to see that look in his eyes.

She forced herself to concentrate on responding to Tiffany. "I would create a fragrance that embodies the heat of the sun for you, something bold and flavorful, with an underlying hint of sweetness, like violets and cassis."

"I don't know what cassis is, but I want it," Tiffany said. "When are you opening your shop?"

"Oh gosh, I'm not even sure I am," she said, though she was getting more excited about the idea by the minute. "I really just made the decision to start thinking about it more seriously."

"If anyone can do it," Carson said, "it's you, Tabs."

"Thank you. It's not the doing it that worries me. It's everything that goes into starting up a business." His support was so nice after so many years of feeling unsupported. She couldn't wait to tell him that the first scent she'd ever created for herself rather than for a company was one that reminded her of him.

She was still tweaking it, and didn't want him to know until she was sure it was perfect.

"I recently opened my office," Tiffany said. "I could help you find space. I worked with Phoebe Nice, one of Dylan's friends. She owns tons of real estate here. I bet she could find you something."

"Wait." Amanda's eyes moved between Carson and Tiffany. "Are you moving here from Paris? Or are you going to open your shop there?"

The room grew silent, and Carson's hand stilled.

"I'm, um. I'm not sure just yet," Tawny managed. Although Carson had told her he wouldn't ask her to leave Adeline, she knew that he wanted her to stay. She'd come here to figure out how to move forward, and now she was more confused than ever. She hadn't thought this far ahead and couldn't imagine leaving Adeline, even for Carson. Even if they tried to have a long-distance relationship, they couldn't do that forever. Maybe thinking about starting a business was the wrong thing to do right now after all.

A wave of disappointment tumbled through her. "I'm leaving late Tuesday to go back to Paris, and I have commitments there, so…"

"Tuesday? That's the day after tomorrow," Tiffany said with an air of disbelief. Her gaze drifted between Tawny and Carson. "Are you coming back?"

Dylan and Brett exchanged serious looks. Tawny and Carson hadn't talked about particulars beyond wanting to be with each other, and everyone was watching her expectantly. She cleared her throat and forced herself to sit up a little straighter, hoping to change the subject.

"I know it's been a really fast trip," Tawny finally responded, laughing nervously. "I don't have it all figured out yet, but I'm glad I got a chance to meet you guys. I haven't had this much fun in a long time."

Amanda smiled warmly. "We're glad you came. But I hate that you're leaving so soon. We didn't get much time together. Tiff and I are meeting for breakfast tomorrow morning. I don't mean to steal you away from Carson, but do you think you can break away for an hour and join us? We can talk about all of this, and you can meet my sister, Ally. She's married to Heath Wild, who grew up with these guys."

Tawny knew all about Heath and his three brothers. Carson had told her stories about how the Wilds had been there for his family when they'd lost Lorelei, and how all eight of the Wild and Bad siblings had been rascally as teens. Although she couldn't imagine Carson getting into much trouble, even as a teenager.

She reached for his hand. They had so little time left together, she didn't want to spend any of it away from him. But she was drawn to these wonderful women, and they'd gotten along so well already, she wanted to spend more time with them, too.

"You'll love Ally," Amanda said. "I hope you'll join us."

Tiffany jumped to her feet, using the remote to turn the volume up on the television. "Halftime's over! Tawny," she said, eyes glued to the television, "you definitely should join us!"

"Are you sure you don't mind if I come along?" Tawny asked, still unsure about missing time with Carson.

"We'd love it," Tiffany said, sitting down beside Dylan. "I grew up with brothers, and Amanda and Ally, and Ally's sisters-in-law, are amazing. I've never had many female friends, and they opened up a whole new world for me."

"She's confused," Dylan said. "That would be *me* who introduced her to a new world. In the *bedroom*."

Everyone laughed.

Tawny realized they were opening up a new world for her, too, with friends who had each other's backs and an openness that might take some getting used to. She had heard so many stories about Carson's brothers, seeing the bond between them and witnessing the love Dylan and Tiffany shared had confirmed her impression of his closely knit, emotional family. She wondered if he and his brothers were that close before their lives were turned upside down, or if that had strengthened their bond. They were obviously raised well by loving parents, despite the breakup of their family.

She suddenly longed for her father, realizing for the first time that she was an *orphan*, like Adeline.

The power of that word sank into her bones, taking her longing even deeper. For the briefest of moments, she allowed herself to fantasize about what it would be like if she moved there and she and Carson gave the relationship all they had. Would they get together with everyone like this often? Or would they fall into the pattern of so many couples, turning into workaholics with the start of her new business and Carson's ongoing firm? He was taking time off now, but she'd never expect that on a day-to-day basis. She was proud of what he'd accomplished, and he wasn't the type of person who could go for long periods without being intellectually stimulated. Would he want his own children? A bigger question was, would he one day be open to fostering children?

She was getting way ahead of herself. She glanced at Tiffany and Dylan, who were watching the game and holding hands. They were a perfect match. *Like me and Carson*. Would she eventually feel comfortable teasing about things like being tied up, too?

As if he could read her mind, Carson pulled her closer and whispered, "I'm glad you're here with me, but I can't wait to get you naked."

She felt her cheeks flame, her gaze darting around the room. No one seemed to be able to tell that he'd set her body on fire.

Carson kissed the tender skin beside her ear. "I do love you, Tabs." He pushed a hand into her hair, holding her ear right beside his mouth. His tongue slid along the shell, and she held her breath. "I can't wait to tie you down and drive you out of your mind."

He leaned back with a sinful look in his eyes as she sat frozen in place, hoping no one had heard him. He was testing her—and as nerve-racking as it was, she didn't want him to stop. She wanted *more*. God, how did he know when to push and when to ease up?

In the next breath, that fierce stare softened, and he kissed her lips, then whispered, "I don't want to miss a minute of our time together. But you should go to breakfast with the girls, or they'll come drag you from my arms in the morning anyway. Tell them you'll go."

She was supposed to answer the girls? To actually *speak* when her body was vibrating as she imagined being tied up on his big, glorious bed, at his mercy.

Tiffany and Amanda laughed at something, snapping her out of her fantasy.

"*Breakfast*," Amanda said. "We were talking about breakfast, remember? Tawny, I'll text you the name of the café and the address. We'll see you at eight?" She pulled out her phone again.

Carson rubbed the back of Tawny's neck, a gratified smile on his lips. That look alone made her want to hear his rough voice taunting her with more dirty promises.

"I have to warn you," Tiffany said, "you might never want to go back to Paris after experiencing the newly formed *breakfast club*. We're pretty awesome."

Breakfast club? If Carson continued surprising her, she might never want to leave his bed.

"Don't you guys have to work?" Brett asked.

"My first meeting is at ten." Tiffany flashed a smile at Tawny. "It's awesome being your own boss. You're going to love it, Tawny."

"I'm sleeping with my boss, and he's out of town, so..." Amanda glanced up from her phone, her cheeks flushed. "I'm kidding. I mean, I am married to my boss, but I don't go in until nine tomorrow. I wouldn't abuse our relationship that way."

Brett shook his head and laughed. "You worry too much, sweetheart. No one here is judging you."

"Thanks, Brett," Amanda said.

"I'm too busy judging Carson for taking off time to be with Tawny," Brett joked.

Tawny felt her eyes widen and tried not to look too alarmed.

"Dude, cut the shit," Carson said. "Tawny doesn't know you well enough to know you're kidding."

Brett leaned forward, elbows on knees, and looked at Tawny with big, brown, apologetic eyes. She bet that sad-puppy look dropped lots of panties.

"Sweetheart, I'm one big-ass joke after another. Carson's the *man*. He can do whatever he wants. I might be his business partner, but he built the company, and it wouldn't be as successful as it is if not for your boyfriend's business savvy and genius mind." Brett shifted his gaze to Carson. "I personally think Tawny should monopolize you for one week each month. You never take time off, and I've never seen you smile as much as you have tonight."

Hearing Brett praise and support Carson made Tawny's chest feel full. One thing was very clear, if she and Carson stayed together, they'd have to live in New York, because there was no way she'd want him to upend his life and miss out on occasions like these. He had so many people who loved him. How did she get lucky enough to have someone so genuinely good fall in love with her?

The girls were awaiting their answer. It had taken Tawny years to come back to Carson, and in just a weekend, he'd made her feel so good, so complete, and even better than her old self. She didn't want to stop there. She wanted to nurture these new friendships and become part of their group. Part of Carson's world. *Regret comes from living your life wearing someone else's skin. It's fixable.*

No more regrets. This time she was going for the brass ring.

She reached for Carson's hand, thankful for his support, and said to the girls, "I would love to meet you for breakfast tomorrow."

CARSON SPENT THE majority of the second half of the game taunting—*testing*—Tawny. They'd never tested each other's boundaries in public before this weekend, and he had a feeling that was the only way to get her to realize that what she felt for him was a good thing and that she could handle it despite her fears. While the others were cheering for touchdowns, Carson set out to get Tawny so hot and bothered, her need for him was inescapable. As the evening wore on, he continued whispering dark promises, brushing against her breasts, rubbing her thighs. She'd been so cute trying to avoid his gropes when she was talking to Amanda. The two of them were so engrossed in conversations about fragrances and Paris he almost felt guilty for his sly maneuvers. But the clock was ticking, and he wasn't going to let her go back to Paris with any doubts in her head.

By the time they left Dylan's, the girls were laughing and hugging like they'd known each other forever. But Tawny's laughter quickly turned to hungry kisses on the way home, and by the time they stumbled into Carson's house they were both out of control. He tore her coat down her shoulders, trapping her arms behind her, and backed her up against the wall, kissing her with all the passion he'd been holding back. She tasted of sweet liquor, seduction, and *Tabby*.

He stripped his coat off, dropping it on the floor, and tore off her pretty new boots and socks—he couldn't have her slipping on the hardwood. He placed them beside her before urgently reclaiming her mouth. A decade of desire flooded out of him, and when he inhaled her oxygen as his own, her essence filled him to the bone. She was delicate and strong, and writhing against him with purposeful taunts of her incredible curves. When she moaned in that sultry, take-me-now way she had, something inside him snapped—and he gave her exactly what she needed.

"How much do you like your sweater?" he growled.

Her wide grin and smoldering eyes gave him his answer. He grabbed the neckline and tore the thick fabric right down the middle. When he grabbed the cups of her bra to tear that off, too, "*Front clasp,*" flew from her lips.

He fumbled with the clasp, shoving the straps down her arms. Her breasts jutted out, tempting and alluring. "You're so fucking sexy. How could you *ever* think I'd need, or want, any other woman?"

She trapped her lip between her teeth. Her sudden shyness was a reminder of what strength it must have taken for her to come to him, to leave her safe life across the sea and face her greatest fears—and desires—that had frightened her into running off in the first place. His heart swelled, and he had the strange urge to build a fortress around her, to protect her from anything ever making her feel uncomfortable again. But that wasn't what she wanted, or what she needed. He knew his beautiful girl, knew what made her feel safe, knew how to take her to new heights every time they made love.

He brushed his lips over hers. "Don't you ever doubt my love for you, baby."

He lowered his mouth over one breast, sucking and teasing as he pinched her other nipple. Tawny went up on her toes, dragging in air between clenched teeth. He opened his eyes, drinking in her exquisite beauty as he drove her wild. Her head was tipped back, eyes closed. Her silky hair fell against the wall like a sunset. Her milky skin was flushed and rosy, and her lips were pink and swollen from their rough kisses. And she was all *his.*

Tawny made a needy sound, drawing his mind back to the pleasures he was bringing her. He shoved her panties and leggings down her thighs and pressed his mouth to her sex, inhaling the exhilarating scent of her arousal. He slid his tongue along her slick heat, clutching her ass.

"Oh *God.*" She whimpered, struggling against the confines

of her coat and leggings, which had trapped her arms behind her and her legs too close together. She pressed her shoulders against the wall, bowing forward.

He loved her this way, *wanting* and *needy*, and thrust his tongue between her legs.

"*Please*, Carson. You teased me all night. I need you inside me."

She tasted too spectacular to rush, and he had a long night of pleasures planned for his lover girl. He pressed his tongue to her clit, teasing over and around her sensitive nerves, applying just the right amount of pressure to bring her up to the brink of release. He held her there until she was so aroused, her essence wet her thighs. He stripped off his pants and pushed his cock between her legs, pumping his hips and sliding along her sex until his shaft was drenched.

"Squeeze me, baby."

Her thighs flexed, squeezing him deliciously. He kissed her deeply as he continued the sensual torture. She moaned into the kiss, and he pumped faster, using his hand to stimulate her.

"Come on my cock, Tabby."

Her breathing came faster as she rose onto her toes, using her shoulders against the wall for leverage as she flexed her thighs and ground her hips. He stood taller, pressing the length of his cock harder along her center as he took her up, up, *up* and devoured her neck. Her eyes slammed shut, and his name burst from her lips. He dropped to his knees, feasting on her sex, catching every pulse of her orgasm. She moaned and panted as her climax rumbled through her.

When she came down from the peak, her body leaned heavy against the wall, her energy drained. He rose and pushed his hands into her hair, and her eyes sprang open. He lowered his mouth to hers, her arousal melting on their tongues. He felt her body stirring to life again.

"Still with me, my sweet, savory Tabby?"

"Yes," she said breathily.

"What do you want, baby?"

"*You*, Carson. I want all of you. *Everywhere.*"

He turned her around, her hands still trapped in her coat behind her back. She rested her cheek against the wall and closed her eyes, sighing the sigh of a woman who'd waited a lifetime for the next moment. Her trust in him never failed to consume him, making him fall deeper in love with her every single day.

"I've got you, baby," he whispered in her ear.

He stripped off her leggings, kissing and caressing her hamstrings, and dragged his tongue along the curve of each cheek before parting the soft globes and licking between them. He slicked his tongue around the rim of her most sacred opening, feeling her clench against him. He continued teasing, licking from one hole to the other, until he felt tension pooling between her legs, wet and tight. He nudged her legs open wider, teasing her puckered flesh with his finger. She moaned, pushing her hips back. *An invitation.* He pushed one finger past the tight rim. Reaching around her hip, he teased her sex with his other hand and placed openmouthed kisses along the base of her spine as he thrust his fingers into her sex, seeking the spot that would make her toes curl. He read her body perfectly, catching every hitch of her breathing, every rock of her hips, every trembling beat of her pulse. He pushed a second finger into her ass and felt her sex clench.

"Relax, baby. Let me in."

When he pushed a third finger in, she cried out, and he

stilled. "Talk to me, Tabby."

"Don't stop," she pleaded.

"That's my greedy girl."

He stripped her coat and bra from her arms, coming out of his sexual haze long enough to realize they hadn't even made it past the foyer. Some part of him felt bad about that, but when she reached behind her, urging him to hurry, she reminded him this wasn't one-sided. He guided her hands to the wall, wet his cock with her slickness, and aligned it with her tightest hole. He pushed the head past the rim, and she inhaled a sharp breath, her fingers curling into the wall for support. He pressed one hand to her belly while the other gripped her shoulder, and he plunged in deep, feeling her entire body shudder and clench. His insides ignited, burning through his core, awakening his very soul as he claimed her in a way he'd never taken another woman. This was theirs, like the rest of their sensual explorations. He was utterly and completely *hers*.

"Oh *God—it'sbeensolong*," she said breathlessly.

He stilled, grinding his teeth together at the thought of hurting her. "Too much?"

"No. *Move*, Carson. *Move*."

He found a fast, hard rhythm, the way he knew they both craved. Groping her breasts, he brought her upright and settled one hand along her neck, feeling her erratic pulse against his fingers.

"*God*, baby," he ground out.

His hand moved down her belly, and he thrust his fingers into her sex. She went up on her toes, scratching at the wall, trying to claim purchase.

"*Carson—*"

"I need your mouth, baby. I want to feel all of you at once."

She craned her neck to the side, and he took her fiercely—*everywhere*. She made a low moaning sound in her throat, and seconds later her body shuddered and quaked, drawing the come right out of him.

"*Fuuuck*—"

He wrapped his arms around her, kissing her shoulders and neck, his heart pouring out of his mouth like lava. "I love you, Tabby. I love you so much I have no idea how I existed on memories for all these years."

She reached up with a trembling hand, her fingers sliding over his cheek to his lips, and he kissed them.

"Carson," she whispered. "Take me to bed."

He lifted her into his arms and carried her upstairs, where he laid her on the bed. He brushed her hair from her face, wondering how a single, delicate person could ground him so completely. He kissed her softly, refusing the voices in his head reminding him that in less than forty-eight hours she'd be gone.

"I'll be back in a sec," he said, and kissed her one last time before heading for the bathroom.

He returned with a washcloth, carefully cleaning her up. She lay with her eyes closed, a sweet smile on her lips. He loved taking care of her after they were intimate, and he felt privileged that she'd always trusted him enough to allow him to do so. He returned to the bathroom and washed up, thinking about the look in her eyes earlier when he'd whispered dirty things at Dylan's house, and how incredible it was to simply be around her again. When he came out of the bathroom, he found Tawny sitting up on her knees in the middle of the bed, one hand between her legs, the other beckoning him closer.

"What's on your mind, sweet girl?"

"*Everything*," she said in a sultry voice.

He stopped in front of the armoire. "As you wish, my greedy girl."

Chapter Eleven

CARSON CROSSED THE dark room like a panther on the prowl, chin low, narrow eyes locked on his prey. *Your very willing and eager prey.* He was sex and love personified, with a body primed for dominance but willing to submit, and an intensely loyal heart that didn't hold Tawny's fears against her. He set the leather box he'd retrieved from the armoire on the bed and unlocked it. Tawny recognized the gold studs at the corners and the marred leather on the side from when she'd accidentally knocked it off the bed when they were in college.

Carson turned the box toward her, revealing a set of dice, the suede-and-cashmere flogger he'd driven her wild with, several lengths of black silk ties, rope, and cashmere-and-leather wrist and ankle cuffs. Heat and lust swirled through her like a hurricane.

"Are those—"

"*Ours*, pretty girl. Never used on anyone else."

She crawled closer, her heart drumming an overwhelming beat as she reached into the box and picked up the dice, eyeing Carson. The weight of them was familiar. Comforting and arousing. One roll of the dice would tell them who was in control tonight. His brows lifted, a secret smile playing on his lips. She closed her fingers around the dice, remembering the first time they'd both relinquished their fate to them. She'd been imagining being bound to his bed, but the idea of *Carson* tied down electrified her.

She gazed into the box again, spotting body oils and lotions, candles, and other paraphernalia they'd toyed with, and she remembered how frightened she'd been at the sight of the flogger he'd bought as a birthday gift for her. She'd thought he was trying to get her to take their lovemaking to a darker level, and she'd been terrified of the idea of the strands of leather slapping against her skin. But she'd had the wrong idea. Carson liked to spank, but only when *she* was into it, and he definitely wasn't into whipping. He was into *sensuality*, not hard-core domination, sadism, or masochism.

She opened her hand, the dice staring back at them like the apple in the Garden of Eden. "Can we…?"

His eyes darkened. "Tawny Bishop, do you want me to submit to you?"

She waggled her brows.

He eyed the box, and she withdrew the flogger, dragging the soft strands of the falls along the length of his arm. The muscles in his jaw tightened, and his now fully erect cock twitched. She couldn't resist brushing the falls along his abs, licking her lips at the eager jump of his shaft.

Standing at the edge of the bed, he grabbed her wrist, drawing her arm away. "I need your mouth on me, Tabs."

He smelled clean and manly, and she wanted his thick cock in her mouth, but she wanted something else more. "Dice," she challenged.

His mouth closed tight, dark eyes boring into her.

She cocked her head, waiting him out.

"I want your mouth on me," he said, more demanding this time. He held his palm up and said, "Lick."

She did, and he wrapped his hand around his cock, giving it several slow, tight strokes. Her desire to win this battle of wills melted a little with each one. She set the dice on the bed and moved her hands between her legs. His gaze turned predatory again. Oh, how she loved that! She set the flogger down and brought her other hand to her breast, teasing her nipple as she fingered her clit. He stroked harder, watching her every move. When a bead formed on the tip of his cock, he arched his brow again. *Loooord*. She wanted it on her tongue. Their eyes connected, and she quickened her pace, feeling the tease of an orgasm.

"Tabby, do you really want me to come like this? Not *on* you? *In* you? *With* you?"

"Dice," she said breathily, hanging on by a thread.

He stopped stroking, his thumb hovering over the bead of white.

"Don't," she begged.

His lips curved up in a wicked grin, and he said, "*Dice*, Tabby."

She let out a breath she hadn't realized she'd trapped. She walked on her knees to the very edge of the bed and pushed her slick fingers into his mouth. "Release *my* cock, please."

He sucked her fingers, holding her gaze as he swirled his tongue around them, and held both hands up. He reached for the dice, and she grabbed his wrist.

"Not yet," she said firmly. He'd given her what she wanted, the chance to roll the dice, but she wanted something else, too—just as much as he did. "If you come, I won't play tonight. So *don't* come, because I have to soon, and you don't want me going home needy, do you?"

He clenched his jaw as she lay on her back and hung her

head off the edge of the bed beside him. She knew he loved this position, as it allowed her to open her throat so she could take him deeper. It had taken her a number of times to learn how to do it properly, and she hadn't done it since they'd broken up. She used to be able to make him come with a squeeze and a tug of his balls in this position, which was why she'd made the threat. She wanted him to know she intended to *win* the toss of the dice and remain in control. Now, as they aligned themselves, her nerves flamed. What if she wasn't good at it anymore?

He leaned over her, one strong hand perched on the edge of the bed, as he dragged the bead over her tongue. "Just for you, Tabby," he said in a heady voice.

His essence spread over her tongue, calming her worries as he entered her mouth slowly, giving her time to adjust to the intrusion. Her body remembered what to do—*just like riding a bike*—and soon he was drilling into her, one hand between her legs, the other keeping his balance. She grabbed his balls, and he groaned, slowing his pace.

"Tabby, you feel too good. I'm going to come."

She closed her teeth around his cock, and he stilled.

"*Fuck*, Tabs. Seriously? How can I not come? Look at you."

She smiled around his cock, and he began moving slowly again.

"You're killing me, baby."

He thrust a few more times, then grabbed the base of his cock and withdrew. He sank down on his knees and replaced his cock with his tongue, thrusting in and out, deep and then shallow, fast and then slow. She reached between her legs, needing an orgasm more than she needed her next breath, but he grabbed her wrist.

"Dice," he commanded.

Damn. How could she argue? She sat up on her knees, and he set the dice in her hand. He wrapped his hand around hers, their eyes connecting, sending silent messages of trust and unspoken boundaries.

"Even," she said shakily, a little nervous about taking this next step. If she rolled an even number, she gained control. If she rolled an odd number, Carson held the reins.

Carson nodded, reminding her of the first time she'd tried to take control. He'd been hesitant and uncomfortable with completely giving up control. She'd wanted it, *needed* it so badly, she'd refused to relent. He'd argued that he was the man, and she'd argued that he sounded like an arrogant asshole. He'd been visibly hurt by that, but it had opened his eyes to what he'd been asking of her, and with a few, more rational, arguments, he'd given in.

He set the box on the floor and waved to the hardwood, his hand fisting and unfisting. His expression hadn't changed, but those long fingers were a giveaway that he wasn't quite as ready as he might have thought. Knowing she wasn't alone in her apprehension made her feel *less* nervous.

"One throw?" She climbed off the bed as he agreed. "Ready?"

His answer came in the form of a squeeze of her hand, a silent nod. She tossed the dice and watched them tumble across the floor. One rolled to a stop by the dresser—*six*—the other rolled beneath the furniture. She and Carson exchanged a glance wrought with anticipation. They both dropped to their hands and knees, peering beneath the dresser. The die sat too far back for her to see. She bit her lip. Carson frowned. And then they both laughed.

"You can reach it," she said, smiling at her ridiculous mistake.

He shook his head. "Only you, Tabby Cat. Only you."

Carson squinted, peering at the die. He drew it forward and scooped it into his big hand. "Looks like I'm all yours, sweetheart."

"Really?" She sounded like she'd just won the sexual lottery. Would it be inappropriate to do a fist pump?

Carson splayed his hands, a sinful grin on his face. Tawny tapped her chin, making the most of the moment—and trying to calm her nerves. She walked around him slowly, as if she were assessing him, when really, her pulse and her thoughts were going crazy.

I won! I won! Oh no! What now?

It had been a decade since she'd done this.

"Where *shall* I start?" she said as saucily as she could.

Carson crossed his arms.

"Uh-uh." She waved her finger. "Arms down, please. I want to check out the merchandise."

"Christ," he mumbled.

She patted his ass, cupped his balls, tweaked his nipple, doing her best to feign confidence that was slowly slipping away. Ten years was a long time, and being in control could be as nerve-racking as handing it over. It took finesse to turn a man like Carson into melted butter. She'd once mastered the skill. What if she wasn't as good at it anymore? The scent of their lust and love hung in the air. She pushed aside her worries, and when that didn't work, she plowed through them. Carson had never let her down; she wasn't about to let him down now.

As she stepped in closer, their body heat spiked. She ran her hands up his neck and into his hair. Carson's chin dropped to his chest with a hiss. He held her gaze as she slowly and purposefully slid her tongue along her lips. His cock rose to the occasion, twitching against her belly. *Guess I'm not so bad after all.*

He pressed his hand to hers. "You're shaking."

"Ten years is a long time," she admitted. "Kiss me, Carson. I need your mouth on mine."

THE VULNERABILITY IN Tawny's eyes contradicted the strength in her voice, and as their mouths came together, Carson felt himself disappearing into her. He dealt with high-powered businesswomen all the time. Women who clung to control like a security blanket and put themselves on a pedestal, expecting the world to do the same simply because they were beautiful, powerful, or a public figure. Tawny was too *real* for any of that nonsense. She accepted control in careful steps, taking and giving and testing her own comfort zones, which was why he had pretended to see the number on the die and relinquished control. She'd wanted this control. He'd seen the hunger in her eyes—just as he'd seen that confidence waver once she had it.

They kissed and groped their way across the floor, tumbling to the bed in a tangle of limbs and passionate noises. Carson fought against his baser instincts to regain control and take what he wanted. It was a constant battle in his mind when it came to Tawny. She brought all of his primal instincts to the surface. He wanted to be her protector, to roar like an idiot and bang his chest around other men and to show her his adoration through wild lovemaking. She was the *only* person who brought out that side of him, and as she rolled on top of him, lacing her fragile fingers with his, he remembered the first time she'd taken control. She'd looked at him like she didn't know where to start, very similar to how she'd looked at him moments earlier. And when she'd blindfolded him, she'd given away her nervousness with every touch, though she'd maintained what he was sure she'd thought had been a look of determination. It had endeared him toward her in a way he hadn't expected, and it was those honest emotions that had spiraled into so much more.

She drew back from the kiss and gazed into his eyes with a lustful, playful expression.

My sweet Tabby has found her courage.

"Think you can behave while I get a few things?" she asked as she rubbed her center along the length of his cock.

"We'll see."

She crawled off the bed and dug around in the box. He ached to be touched, and fisted his cock, giving it a few tight tugs. She set the wrist cuffs and silk ties on the bed, and he jerked himself a few more times.

"You are a very naughty boy," she said.

"Use the rope," he ground out, wanting the sting that came with it when he struggled.

"I'm the boss tonight, *mister.*" She leaned over the bed and kissed his stomach, watching his hand slide along his cock. "Aren't you the eager beaver? I should flip you over so you get none of that pleasure for misbehaving. Although…" Her eyes narrowed seductively. "I could watch you do that all day long."

He swallowed hard, knowing she was building ideas in her pretty little head. "Tabby Cat," he said sternly. "Rope, *please.*"

Her shoulders dropped and she grabbed two lengths of rope and stood at the end of the bed. She held one of his ankles, watching him as she wound the rope around it. A stab of insecurity he hadn't felt in years sliced through him, mixed with the insatiable need for what she was doing. It wasn't sexual insecurity, but because in this position he couldn't protect or help her if she got hurt. Those fears burned inside him, and as he'd learned to do, he focused on the grating of the rope against his skin, the spreading of his legs as she tightened the tension on the second rope.

"I think I need to gag you if you're going to be demanding, but then I'd lose out. Your mouth is worth dealing with a little bossiness." She yanked the rope tighter, spreading his legs farther apart.

Damn, he'd missed the sensation of his skin being pulled too tight, and the sheer anticipation of *Tawny Bishop*. She bound one of his wrists, and when he placed his free hand up for her, she shook her head.

"Don't stop what you were doing, but don't come, either."

"Tabs," he said too harshly, but the pressure and heat were already pounding through him. "That's going to be near impossible. It's been too long since we've done this."

She crouched beside the bed, and when she appeared again, she held a bottle of flavored lube. She drizzled the cool liquid along his cock and put her mouth beside his ear, whispering, "Do it for me."

With a low growl, because *damn it*, there was nothing he wouldn't do for her, he began stroking his cock. The slick friction sent a bolt of lightning shooting through him. Tawny dragged a length of silk over his pecs, amping up his pleasure.

"Close your eyes."

Her tone told him she was in serious play mode. She secured the silk over his eyes, and he felt her nimble fingers securing it on the side of his head as he'd taught her. His temperature spiked with the absence of sight, and his other senses prickled to life. He heard the bottle of lube open again, and tensed, readying for the cool liquid to hit his skin, but it never did. The bed dipped beside him, and Tawny's soft, pillowy lips pressed against his, kissing him deeply and pulling a needy moan from his lungs. *Fuck*, everything she did turned him inside out. When her hand cupped his balls and squeezed, her fingers slippery with lube, his body clenched and his cock jumped in his hand, reminding him she'd wanted to watch. Holy fuck, the image of her eyes on his cock and the feel of her hands as she gave his balls a tug nearly made him lose it. He gripped the base of his shaft, groaning.

She drew back, tickling his balls with her fingertips. "Too much?"

The sassiness in her voice made him smile, but he was right on the verge of coming, and he ground that smile into another sound of restraint. Her hand moved over his, circling his cock, her slippery fingers sliding between his as she guided them slowly up and over the head.

"Tabs—" His words got lost as he panted, clinging to his control, and his ability to think, by a shred.

She left him then, off the bed, silent in her disappearance. He held the base of his erection, listening intently, but the air held no clues to her whereabouts. It had been so long, he'd forgotten what it felt like to be left in this situation—and it reminded him of the night they'd broken up. His heart physically hurt with the memory. He fisted his hand in the sheet, clenched his jaw, *willing* it away, and then her hand captured his, drawing it up and over his head as she bound it with the rope, distracting him from his distress. The feathery falls of the flogger glided up his leg, over his hip, and across his chest, bringing rise to goose bumps. *Lower, baby. Drag that sucker along my cock like your hair.* As quickly as it had touched his skin, it was gone again.

Christ, she knew him too well to satisfy him that easily.

The room was quiet again, save for the sound of his own harsh breathing. Then her hot mouth was on his balls, sucking one in completely. The bed dipped between his legs, and her slippery fingers touched his ass, teasing the rim.

"Holy *fuck*, Tabby."

Her other hand gripped his cock, stroking him as she sucked his balls, and she pushed a finger into his ass. He cried out with the invasion, but she didn't relent, seeking the spot that would make him come like a fountain. She sucked harder, stroking him tight and fast. Lust spiked down his spine, pooling at the base and spreading to his groin like a five-alarm fire as she breached his rim over and over again. He struggled against the ropes, trying to bite back his orgasm, but there was no relief, and when she hit the perfect spot, his legs flexed. Sparks zinged through him as he exploded in streaks of hot come across his chest and stomach. She continued licking and sucking as he writhed beneath her control, moaning and grunting through the very last of his release.

And then she disappeared again, leaving him alone to listen and try to calm his breathing.

He might be alone in the room, but for the first time in a decade, he knew he wasn't truly alone.

Chapter Twelve

TAWNY WASHED UP and returned to the bedroom with a warm, wet washcloth. Her heart hammered against her ribs at the sight of her powerful man blindfolded and bound to the bed, his body glistening with the proof of his arousal. His scent lingered in the air, like a Callery pear tree. The emotions thrumming through her, the immense love she had for Carson, were so powerful, she couldn't speak. She bathed him in silence, soaking in the sound of his breathing, the feel of his body, the small smile on his lips. When she put the washcloth in the bathroom and came back to him, she ran her fingers from his ankle to his hips, along his torso, and climbed onto the bed next to him. She lay on her side, tracing his jaw with her fingertips, then with kisses, deciding what to do next. Every inch her fingers covered brought a sense of completeness, of awe over his beauty and his strength. How many men would allow this? she wondered. Her thigh slid over his, and when his lips parted, she traced those, too.

"Baby," he breathed out.

She moved over him, her legs between his, and untied his blindfold. He blinked several times, and as the fog of darkness cleared, his eyes filled with heat, and he went hard beneath her.

"Tabby Cat. What you do to me…"

The wonder in his voice brought his words to life, and she

felt the depth of them everywhere—on her skin, in her heart, in the very air she breathed. She caressed his cheeks, and his eyes fluttered closed. The softness of his skin and the feathery flutter of his long lashes contradicted his corded muscles, drawing her heart closer to the surface. She knew there could never be another man in her life. She felt on the verge of tears, admitting to herself what she'd probably known all along. When he sighed, she touched his lips, bringing his eyes open again.

"I love you, Carson, with my whole heart."

He craned his neck up, and she met him in a warm, loving kiss. She needed to be in his arms again.

She untied his ankles, rubbing them, working her way up his calves with kisses, easing the tension from his muscles and seeing it rise elsewhere. Her body prickled with heat again. She crawled onto the bed, and his powerful legs closed around her, locking her against him.

"I was going to untie you, but suddenly I want to play."

"You should have untied my arms first so I could hold you."

She pressed her finger over her lips. "Soon."

Wiggling out from between his legs, she straddled his torso. "First, I'm feeling a little needy."

That earned a hungry grin, and when she leaned forward, brushing her breast over his lips, he eagerly gave her what she wanted. She closed her eyes, reveling in the incredible sensations. She grabbed hold of his arms, using them for leverage as she offered him her other breast. He took it between his teeth, his eyes locked on hers, and he bit down. She cried out, wincing against the pleasure and pain.

"Good *Lord*, Carson. I felt that *everywhere*."

"I need more of you. Get up here and let me make you come." His wolfish grin and demanding voice made her laugh.

Why did his sexual frustration turn her on so much? "My, my…"

"Tabby." His brows knitted and a serious scowl formed on his handsome face. "Get over here and let me taste you, *please*."

She lowered her face so their mouths were a breath apart, unable to stop smiling. "What woman in her right mind would deny you that pleasure?"

"Don't you dare," he said.

She moved down his body, sliding her sex over his erection, and lowered her mouth to his pecs, teasing him as he did her. Her hands traveled over his flesh as she increased the friction between her legs, moving faster, needing more.

"Tabby, I don't want to come unless I'm inside you."

She rose on her knees and guided the head of his cock inside her, moving ever so slightly, not allowing him to enter her fully. His hips rose off the mattress, but she was too quick, lifting herself higher, keeping full penetration at bay.

"Tabs," he warned.

"You're sexy when you're frustrated."

She giggled and climbed up his body again, kissing him hard, then easing to a languid, sensual kiss. His hips undulated as he ground his cock against her, causing her fingers to curl around his arms. *God*, she needed him as badly as he wanted her. She reached between their bodies, rubbing her fingers over her sex; then she slid them into his mouth.

"Mm," he moaned. His eyes went dark as coal. "Not enough."

She moved off of him and stepped from the bed.

"Hey, babe? You're going in the wrong direction."

She began unshackling his wrists. "Sometimes we *both* need more."

The second his hands were untied he swept her beneath him and captured her mouth in a kiss that sang through her veins, making her *ache* and *melt* at once. She would be happy staying right here beneath him, enveloped by his body and entranced by the velvety warmth of his mouth forever. His hands pushed beneath her, cradling her tight against him. Her legs wound around his waist, and he entered her in one fluid motion. Her head fell back against the pillow with the magnificent force of their bodies.

"Carson…" She grasped for the right words to express how she felt.

He touched his forehead to hers, and she knew no words were necessary. Their bodies moved in perfect sync, falling into a warm, sweet rhythm. Tawny felt transported *into* him, as if their beings had become one. Big, strong hands moved down her back and gripped her hips, angling them up and holding her there as he thrust faster, drove in deeper. Their bodies were slick with sweat, their erratic heartbeats creating a pulse-pounding chorus to their gasps and pleas. Her senses reeled, her thoughts skidded, and her desires grew to explosive proportions, and when Carson gazed into her eyes, everything stilled.

"How will I ever let you go back to Paris without me?" Carson whispered. "You are my very heart and soul."

His mouth came tenderly down over hers as he loved her the way only he knew how, and the rest of the world fell away.

Chapter Thirteen

MONDAY ROLLED IN with sunny skies and higher temperatures, melting much of the winter wonderland that had cocooned the city. She and Carson made plans to go to Greenwich Village after she met Tiffany, Amanda, and Ally for breakfast. He said there was a shop he wanted to take her to, though he wouldn't give her any hints about exactly what type of shop it was. Tawny hated leaving him, but she was excited to see the girls again. Carson insisted on having Barton drive her to the café despite her protests, reminding her of when they were in college and he'd walked her out to her car after they were done studying and had made her promise to text him and let him know she'd arrived home safely. Was that another signal she'd missed? How many study partners were that watchful? It still bothered her that she'd missed so many of Carson's signals all those years ago, but she was determined to have more open and honest communication this time around.

I think I was pretty clear last night. Heat spread through her like a gust of wind with memories of their passionate night. The car stopped in front of the café. *Perfect.* As if she wasn't nervous enough, now she was hot and bothered, too.

She inhaled a few calming breaths as Barton opened the door for her. The now-familiar scent of his cologne greeted her as she stepped onto the sidewalk. She liked Barton. He was kind, with wise eyes and a quiet nature, and reminded her of her father.

He handed her a business card and said, "Text me when you're ready to leave and I'll pick you up."

"Thank you, but I might do a little shopping before coming home. I don't mind taking a cab." They weren't far from the Biology Café. She wanted to go by and take a peek and pick up something nice for Carson on the way.

Barton lowered his chin in a very *Carson-like* way, his lips curving up in a knowing smile. "Shopping is not a problem. I'll be ready when you text."

She felt very *Pretty Woman*, and tried not to laugh. Carson was so laid-back with her, but boy, he wasn't kidding about pulling out all the stops. "Thank you, Barton. I'll text you."

Carson was working from home, and she sent him a quick text before heading into the café. *Thank you for putting Barton at my beck and call, but you do remember that I came from nothing, right? Xo*

She tucked her phone into her coat pocket and walked into the café, spotting Tiffany and Amanda and a beautiful dark-haired woman who looked too much like Amanda not to be her sister, Ally, sitting at a table by the window. Her phone vibrated, and she smiled at Carson's name on her screen and read the text. *So did I. We're made for each other. Have fun with the girls. You can thank me properly later.*

Amanda waved her over, and Tawny put away her phone. Carson had texted her a few minutes after she'd left to say Mick had invited them to lunch tomorrow. She was excited to meet the brother who had helped him through the roughest time of his life. He was lucky to have had him when they'd lost their sister. She'd have given anything to have a sibling to reach out to when she'd lost her father. *And every day since.*

Her stomach twisted nervously as she approached the table. Amanda rose to greet her with open arms, embracing her as if they'd known each other forever, instantly putting her at ease.

"Hi," Amanda said. "I'm so glad you made it."

"Thanks for inviting me. Sorry I'm late." She slipped out of her coat and draped it on the back of the chair.

"You're not late. We were early," Tiffany said.

"It's all my fault." The pretty brunette smiled up at Tawny, flashing pearl-white teeth and mischievous eyes. "Hi. I'm Ally, Mandy's sister. I forced her to get up early and go to a yoga class with me this morning."

"And I called Tiffany and dragged her butt out of bed," Amanda explained. "We went home to shower and change afterward, but we were all ready early, so we had a cup of coffee while we waited. You didn't miss anything other than us talking about your sexy romance with the quietest Bad boy of them all."

She was already the center of gossip?

The waitress came and took their orders, and when she left, Tiffany said, "For the record, I said we should call you, but both of them nixed it. Honestly, I don't know what I was thinking by suggesting it."

"Oh, well, that's okay," Tawny said uncomfortably.

"Seriously," Tiffany added. "You're leaving *tomorrow* afternoon. You need *all* the sex you can get before then. It's bad enough that we're stealing you away *now*, but if we don't, who knows when we'll have another chance to really get to know you."

Tawny sighed with relief that she wasn't being excluded.

"*Or* when we'll get the scoop on Carson!" Ally added.

Amanda glared at her.

"What?" Ally said with a laugh. "You know you're dying to know about him. He's so mysterious."

Tawny's stomach fluttered hearing them talk about Carson like they didn't know him at all. As she listened to them talk about how he was always working and when they went out for drinks together he'd never hit on women or brought a woman with him, she felt a sense of warmth and happiness engulf her. He'd been honest about everything.

Wasn't he always?

After the waitress brought her coffee, she decided to find out just how much they knew about Carson. "I can see why he seems mysterious," she said, "but he's never been that way to me. What do you find mysterious about him?"

The three girls exchanged a curious glance.

"Everything," Tiffany said. "From what Dylan tells me, he works all the time and goes running with him a few times a week, but Dylan makes it sound like Carson is otherwise pretty closed off. He said Carson doesn't talk to any of them about women. Like, *ever.*"

"I've worked for Mick for several years, and when Carson comes by the office, he's a complete gentleman, very reserved and proper," Amanda said. "I thought he was like that because our office is so professional, but Brett barges in hitting on Sophie, joking around with everyone, and Carson never has. Is he that serious all the time?"

"That's such a hard question to answer. He's a pretty serious guy in general," Tawny said honestly. "But he has a playful side, and a great sense of humor. At least with me. I mean, I get what you're saying. He's never been the type of guy to brag about what he does with women. If anything, he used to downplay it." Memories of their study sessions came rushing back. *Do you have a girlfriend yet?* she'd asked a few weeks into their friendship. She used to tease him with "yet" because he'd laugh it off every time and say something like, *Not going to happen, Tabs.* "I think he's too confident and in control to brag about anything."

"Sounds like Heath." Ally sighed dreamily. "There's nothing better than a man who's confident and knows what he likes."

"My sister is talking about *in the bedroom.*" Amanda rolled her eyes.

"In *and* out of the bedroom." Ally lowered her voice and said, "I mean, who has sex *only* in the bedroom?"

Tawny felt her cheeks flame. She was surprisingly anxious to jump into their conversation about sex, and equally nervous about doing so. It dawned on her that she and Carson had definitely not had vanilla sex last night, and she wasn't panicking about the girls finding out. Maybe it was because they were talking so openly, or maybe it was because she really had changed.

"*Before* Ally got together with Heath, she had a thing for one-night stands. I was just the opposite," Amanda explained. "I was petrified that something bad was going to happen to her, and then she found the man of her dreams."

"I'm a lucky woman," Ally said. "Heath and I met at a conference. We were supposed to be a one-night stand, but you can't dodge Cupid's arrow. And then Little Miss Wig and Mask here"—she motioned to Amanda—"followed in my footsteps and found her true love."

Tawny looked at Amanda. "'Wig and mask'? Do I even want to know?"

"Hell, yes, you want to know," Tiffany said. "Her story is ten times better than me showing up wearing nothing but a jacket and heels to surprise Dylan and accidentally flashing his brothers *and* the Wilds. If that wasn't enough, I fell bare-ass up in front of *Brett*."

Tawny stifled a laugh. "No!"

The waitress brought their breakfasts, and after she walked away, Tiffany said, "It's the truth. It was definitely not my best moment."

"Maybe not, but you're fierce," Amanda said. "Tiffany owned it when she met them all face-to-face. Carson didn't tell you?"

"No," Tawny said, but it didn't surprise her. "I'm sure he probably blocked it from his mind out of respect for Tiffany and Dylan. He's not a gossiper. But I really want to know about the wig and mask. That sounds intriguing." *Do you use them in the bedroom? Role-play?* Maybe they had more in common than she thought.

Amanda went on to explain how her sister's relationship with Heath had inspired her to try to step outside of her comfort zone. She'd studied a book on seduction and had gone to a masquerade bar crawl to put her newfound talents to the test—and she'd accidentally tested them on her boss. *Mick.*

"It turned out we'd both been in love with each other for a long time, and we went for it," Amanda explained. "I've never been happier. Hey, you guys were really close in college, right? That's what Mick told me. Is that how it was for you and Carson? Or were you just friends before now?"

They were so open and nonjudgmental, the truth came easily. "We were really close friends throughout college, and for almost two years, we were more." She felt like a thousand pounds lifted from her shoulders, but that didn't stop her nerves from whirling like a tornado.

"I knew it!" Amanda said. "Mick and his brothers are so frigging loyal, and when they fall in love, they fall forever. The way Carson was looking at you last night? Tawny, you are one lucky woman."

Knowing they saw the same emotions in the way Carson looked at her as she did made her warm all over.

"Then you're definitely moving here, right?" Tiffany asked. "We can help you find space for your perfumery."

"Mandy and Tiff told me you were going to make personalized fragrances," Ally said. "That's the coolest idea ever. I definitely want to get on your list. Will you do colognes for men? Can we get one for Heath, too?"

Tiffany pulled out her phone. "I'll reach out to Phoebe Nice right now and put you two in touch."

"Wait, you guys…" Overcome with emotions, Tawny felt her eyes dampen with unexpected and confusing tears.

"Oh no, did we say something wrong?" Amanda asked.

"No," she said, trying to regain control, but her feelings came tumbling out. "I'm just…I spent years trying not to think of Carson, and being with him again is even better than I ever expected. Our connection is so deep, it's like all those missing years, and my marriage, never existed. But I don't think I can open a shop here. There's a little girl in Paris, an orphan named Adeline, and I love her so much. I can't just leave her. But even the thought of not being with Carson kills me. And now there's you guys to consider. I have never had friends like you, and overnight you just opened your arms and let me in. I feel like it's all a dream and I'm going to wake up back in Paris alone again."

"A little girl? Are you thinking of adopting her?" Tiffany asked.

"I wish I could, but no. It wouldn't be fair. I work too

much, and I'm single, and I'm also orphaned now, so I have no family support. But I'm not ready to move away from her. I really want to stay in Paris until she's adopted. I need to know that she's safe and happy with a loving family."

Amanda touched her arm. "Tawny, even if you go back to Paris, you'll never be alone again. We're here for you. But how can you leave Carson? Will he move away from his family? Have you talked about it?"

Oh God. She could never ask him to do that.

"Um. Am I the only one who picked up on the word 'marriage'? You were married before?" Ally arched a brow.

Tawny could kick herself for letting that slip. *Mick and his brothers are so frigging loyal, and when they fall in love, they fall forever.* Would they think less of her for having run from her feelings? Should she tell them the truth, or try to play it off in some other way? One look at the empathy in their eyes brought more of the truth.

"Yes. I'm divorced now. In college, Carson and I weren't a couple. Not in the traditional sense, anyway," she admitted. "No one knew about us, and we didn't date, or go to parties together. I had to keep up my grades for my scholarship, and on weekends I tutored kids who were in foster care. I was pretty introverted back then. My friends were bookworms and lab rats. I didn't have girlfriends who talked about things like sex, and I grew up with just my dad. You don't talk about sex with your father. And Carson? Gosh, you guys, he *is* the most amazing person I've ever known. But he told me when we first met that he'd never settle down with one woman. So when we started sleeping together I never thought to push it. For almost two years, we had a *secret* sexual relationship. Things between me and Carson were so hot, I'm surprised we didn't combust. And after a while, he was all I thought about. Being with him, in his arms. In his *bed*. At the same time, I was terrified that people would find out about what we did, because we were…*creative*."

Her cheeks burned, and she waved her hands, laughing nervously. "Anyway, I couldn't handle feeling so out of control. Right before graduation I broke it off with Carson, and a few months later I married a *safe*, boring guy. When my father died, it all came to a head. I ended my loveless marriage and took off to Paris to find myself." Her gaze drifted around the table. The compassion in their eyes made her feel *safe* enough to tell them the rest of the story. "But how could I find myself when a part of me still belonged to Carson?"

Amanda and Tiffany said, "Aw," in unison.

"You poor thing," Ally said. "You needed better friends for sure. No wonder Amanda said you and Carson couldn't keep your hands off each other."

Tawny was kind of relieved they'd noticed. Hiding wasn't something she wanted to do anymore. And she knew that just because they recognized affection didn't mean they knew what happened behind closed doors.

"Ally! Sorry, Tawny. I meant it in the very best way. What you described? That's true love," Amanda said. "That's *how* you know. I know it's overwhelming to have the three of us ready to blaze a path with you. I've always been reserved and private, more like you than Tiff and Ally. But you can trust us, Tawny. Whether you take baby steps with that trust, or dive right in. Either way, I meant what I said yesterday about adopting you into our sisterhood. It's obvious you and Carson are together for the long haul, even if long-distance, and we'll be here for you, too."

CARSON'S CELL PHONE rang, and he snagged it from his desk, where he'd been poring over a contract in his home office. Mick had called earlier to tell him he'd be back later that evening, and they'd made plans to get together for lunch tomorrow so Mick could finally meet Tawny. He had been the only person Carson had opened up to after Tawny had broken things off. He trusted Mick with his life, but he'd only confessed his heartbreak over Tawny because his brother had seen him locking himself away from the world again and he'd refused to stand idly by and let that happen. He'd ridden Carson until he'd confessed, and Mick had once again been there for him, listening, trying to help figure things out.

Brett's name flashed on the screen. *Talk about going from one extreme to the other.*

"What's up?" Carson answered, hoping there wasn't an issue at the office.

"Considering I'm at work, what's *up* is not what I'd like to be *up*." Brett laughed at his own innuendo.

Carson shook his head. He was used to Brett's humor, but he wasn't in the mood for it today. Tawny had been gone only a few hours, and he missed the hell out of her. How would he get through weeks at a time when she was in Paris? They'd successfully skirted the issue of where they would go from here. He wasn't anywhere near ready for her to leave. And he knew he never would be.

"Hey? No laugh?" Brett asked.

"Just busy. What's going on? Is there an issue at the office?"

"No. I wanted to make sure you were okay."

Carson leaned back against the soft leather chair. "I'm fine. Why?"

"Why?" Brett said incredulously. "Dude, the woman who

you've been madly in love with since college just appeared in your life out of nowhere, and she's leaving *tomorrow*. She didn't answer last night when the girls asked her about coming back. I'm worried about you, bro. I've never seen you like you are with her."

"How did you know how I felt about her in college when I didn't even know? You were even more wrapped up in nonsense then than you are now."

"Seriously? I can check out tits and ass at the same time I'm taking in everything around me. You know that."

Carson smiled. "Yeah, I do. But you're not really a touchy-feely guy. And what the hell do you know about love?"

"Nothing, but I know you. You're harder to crack than a coconut. But when you're with Tawny? When she came to your door in college that time I was visiting with Mom and Dad? Man, one look at you two together was all I needed to know something was up. Around her you're soft as butter."

Carson sighed, surprised he was that easy to read. *Or hard as steel* was on the tip of his tongue, but he knew better than to give Brett that kind of line to run with.

"It's a good thing, right?" Brett asked. "She's back in your life. You're more relaxed, happier."

"Yeah. It's complicated, but it's good. It's amazing, actually."

"I wasn't kidding when I said you should go back to Paris with her. I can manage the operations here for however long you need me to."

"Thanks. I appreciate that. But you and I know it's a much bigger deal than handling a few phone calls. One thing's for sure. I'm not making the mistake of letting her go again."

A call beeped through, and Tawny's name appeared on the

screen. "Thanks for worrying, bro, but we'll figure this out. I've got to take this call."

"Okay, cool. I'm here if shit goes south."

"Thanks." Carson switched over to Tawny's call, his nerves strung tight. "Hey, babe, are you having fun?"

"Carson," she said in a trembling voice.

He bolted to his feet. "What's wrong?"

"The Biology Café is *gone*. I met the girls around the corner and decided to come by and see it, but it's closed. Empty. There's no sign saying it moved or anything." She exhaled loudly. "I just can't believe it's gone."

"Oh, baby. I'm so sorry. I'm coming to get you. Stay there."

"What if this is a sign?"

Fuck. "It's not a sign, Tabs. There are no *signs*. That's something people say when they need false hope, or to rationalize what they're doing." As he said the words, his own claim came back to him. *You coming back to me on the night of the fundraiser? That is important. A sign even.* Goddamn it. Maybe he wasn't as rational as he thought, because that *did* feel like a sign, but this? No fucking way. He wasn't going to lose her over a failed café.

"Tabby, sweetheart, listen to me. I love you and you love me, and a closed café has no bearing on that. I'm going to call Barton and head over. I'll be there in a few minutes."

After talking with Tabby, he called Barton, shoved his feet into his boots, and grabbed his leather bomber jacket. While he waited for Barton to arrive, he made a few more calls to find out what happened to the café. If Tawny was looking for signs, he'd sure as hell find the right one.

Chapter Fourteen

TWENTY MINUTES LATER Carson stood outside the empty retail space that was once the Biology Café with a heartbroken Tawny tucked beneath his arm.

"I don't even know when it closed," she said sadly. "This is the first time I've been back since my father died."

He gazed into her sad green eyes, feeling her sorrow as his own. After losing her father, she must feel like losing the traditions she'd once counted on were like losing pieces of herself all over again. Did she worry that those memories would be forgotten? Or was it bigger than that? Did she feel like parts of herself were being erased?

Whatever was going on in Tawny's head Carson wasn't about to let happen.

"The café was just a symbol, Tabs. Symbols are meaningful on a deep level, but on the surface they're just symbols. If you took away the symbol H_2O, water would still exist, right? Everyone in the world knows that water is a substance, but not everyone knows that H_2O represents it." He waved toward the empty retail space. "That café was your symbol, but what happened here, on this corner, will never change, regardless of the landscape. This corner, this spot on earth, will always be here. That retail space may not be a café, but you'll have this area to come back to, to celebrate your parents' love for each other. I'll set up a table for us right here every year, and we'll have a beautiful lunch in memory of your parents on the anniversary of the day they met. We won't let your traditions be forgotten. I promise you that."

A radiant smile reached all the way up to her eyes. "Is there anything you won't do for me?"

He cradled her face in his hands, vaguely aware of people walking around them, glad she was smiling again. "No. You can count on me, Tabs. You always could. Nothing has changed for the worse, and everything has changed for the better. And right now we're going to get out of here and get your mind off of this." He guided her to the car and asked Barton to take them to Greenwich Village.

"Don't you find it weird that the café closed after my dad died?" she asked. "Like it was meant to be the end to an era, or something? Like I'm supposed to move past it?"

"No, I don't think you're supposed to move past anything. Celebrating your parents' love made you happy. This is a coincidence, that's all. Not a sign," he assured her. "We can't control the variables around us. You know that. We are the only constants in our lives, and some days we can't even control ourselves."

"We can't control them, but we can appreciate them." She pulled a small black velvet bag out of her pocket and set it in his hand. "Even though you're technically a variable, in my heart, you've always been my constant, Carson. It was thoughts of you that drove me to discover the *real me* back in college, and again now. And I'm one hundred percent convinced that thoughts of being with you again were what pulled me through my father's death."

He slid a hand beneath her hair and pulled her into a warm,

sensual kiss. "Thank you, baby, but you don't need to buy me anything. You're here with me, and that's all I've ever wanted." He opened the bag and out dropped a silver necklace with a lowercase, italic *h* charm.

"It's Planck's constant," she said excitedly. "A physical constant that is the quantum of action, central in quantum mechanics. And quantum mechanics is the body of scientific laws that describe the strange behavior of photons, electrons, and the other particles that make up the universe. In my universe, you are my Planck's constant, which explains all of my wacky behavior."

He laughed, but his heart felt like it might crawl out of his chest. He drew her into another kiss, his throat thickening with emotions. "Only you would ever think of something like this, and it's only one of a million reasons why I adore you. Thank you, Tabs."

"I wasn't sure if you'd wear a necklace, and it's okay if you don't want to. I just wanted you to have it. I went with a knife-edge chain, which is very masculine, and—" She stopped explaining as he put it on and tucked it beneath his shirt.

"It's from you," he said. "It'll never come off."

"That makes me so happy," she said softly, and embraced him.

"You're leaving tomorrow. I need to know what you want, Tabs. Do you want to try to build a life with me?"

A sweet, nervous laugh escaped, and she drew in a deep breath. "It's a big jump."

"No, babe. A big jump is marrying someone you're not in love with to escape your fears. Giving up what made you feel complete because you were afraid took far more courage than this will take. You've accepted your sexuality; you've accepted me. What's left to fear?"

She shrugged one shoulder. "I don't know, but I'm not afraid of how I feel anymore. I can't ask you to move away, and I can't move here, Carson. I'm just not ready to leave Adeline for good. I know that might sound crazy, because she's not my daughter, but…"

"Then we'll figure it out so you don't have to. I'll come to Paris. I can't move there full-time, but I can be there for the majority of the time. I'll help you open your business and make connections, and we'll figure it out together," he assured her. "All of it. Tell me you want that."

"But your business and your family…?"

Barton pulled over at the curb and stepped from the car. He opened the back door, and cold air swept over them, but Carson didn't move.

"I'll open an office in Paris. It'll take time and I'll have to put new systems in place, find staff there. But I'll figure it out, and I'll see my family when I come back. I'm *all in*, Tabs. I want to figure us out. The question is, do you?"

She held his gaze, her eyes brimming with adoration as she touched the center of his chest, pressing against the charm she'd given him. "How can I not? You're my constant."

TAWNY WAS SURE she was existing in some sort of dream world, and at some point her hopes, and all this exquisite love she was feeling, would implode and she'd be blown to smithereens. She and Carson had lunch at a cozy restaurant and spent the day knocking around Greenwich Village, checking out cool shops and people watching. He'd wanted to know all about her breakfast with the girls and was happy it had gone well. He was so attentive and genuinely interested, it made her even more excited about their decision to try to figure out a way to make a long-distance relationship work. She must have asked him a hundred times if he was sure he'd want to spend the majority of his time in Paris, and he hadn't hesitated when answering. *If you're in Paris, I'm in Paris.* She was excited and nervous about their plans, but she'd been searching for so long and she finally felt like she was heading in the right direction.

"Ready for your surprise?" Carson asked when they turned a corner. He patted her ass and pointed to a comic book store.

Tawny gasped. "Oh my gosh! I haven't been to a comic book store since college."

"Remember that comic shop near school?" he asked.

"The one where the girl hit on you every time we went in?" she asked, remembering how much she'd hated the feeling of watching the salesgirl check him out.

"She did not."

Tawny rolled her eyes. "Even you were not that oblivious."

As they climbed the steps to the shop he said, "We found that place a few weeks after you and I started sleeping together. Do you really believe I was thinking about some nobody behind a counter instead of the sexy, beautiful woman who was in my bed on a weekly basis?"

She stopped on the top step, with Carson one step below, bringing her closer to his height. "How did I miss so much back then?"

"I think it has something to do with all the amazing sex we were having. You couldn't think straight. Isn't that what you told me?" He kissed her, and the door to the shop swung open. His arm circled her waist, and he tugged her against him, allowing two people dressed in Star Trek costumes to walk past.

They walked inside, and a line of people went around the far wall, leading to a door at the back of the shop, out of which three more people dressed in costumes appeared. The store smelled like musty books and latex. Not an appealing combination. She stepped closer to Carson and buried her nose in his jacket. *Mm. Much better.*

"The line for costumes is against that wall," the bearded guy behind the counter said.

"Costumes for...?" Carson asked.

The guy handed him a flyer, and Tawny quickly scanned the announcement. "There's a science fiction festival at a hotel nearby? Did you know about this, Carson?"

"No. I just wanted to take you to a comic book store like old times."

Her eyes lit up. "We *have* to go! Look, they're showing the movie *Serenity* tonight."

"Sure, but I'm not dressing up in a costume."

"Dude, read the flyer again." The guy behind the counter shook his head. "No costume, no entry."

Tawny beamed at Carson, who looked like he was being asked to swallow a worm.

"Please?" She bounced on her toes and went for sultry, caressing his cheek. "You'd look hot in a costume. *Any* costume."

He laughed. "Tabs, we can watch *Serenity* at my place." He leaned down and whispered, "Naked."

"As enticing as that sounds, I've always wanted to go to Comic Con, and I was always too shy. This is smaller, and *right here*. Look, it says they're hosting new comic book designers, having a costume contest, and selling all sorts of sci-fi paraphernalia."

185

His expression didn't change.

She didn't often try to use her feminine wiles to get her way, but how could she resist a science fiction festival *in costume*? She stepped in so close she could see each whisker on his chin. "I guess we found something you won't do for me."

"Oh, man," the guy behind the counter uttered.

Carson cocked his head to the side, his gaze softening. "Tabs."

His phone vibrated with a call, and he pulled it from his pocket. "Baby, I've got to take this. I'm sorry. Look around at the comics. I'll just be a few minutes." He had gotten several phone calls already. She worried she was keeping him from something important, but he'd assured her earlier that it was nothing he couldn't handle by phone.

"Okay. I'll get in line." She fluttered her lashes flirtatiously and sauntered into line, hoping she could convince him to wear a costume after his call.

He gave her a narrow-eyed look that told her he wasn't happy with her decision, but she'd had to come *way* out of her comfort zone to get up the courage to come to New York and see him in the first place. Now it was his turn. Besides, seeing Carson in a sexy costume would be worth listening to him complain about it.

Fifteen minutes later Tawny was nearing the front of the line and Carson was still outside. She glanced out the window and saw him pacing, the phone pressed to his ear, one hand rubbing the back of his neck. His *nothing* was definitely *something*.

Her cell phone vibrated, and she pulled it from her pocket. Smiling, she opened and read the message from Amanda. *Mick said you're coming by the office tomorrow to meet him. I can't wait to see you again!* Tawny was excited to see Amanda again, too. She sent a quick reply—*Me too! And I'm excited to meet Mick, too!*

Her phone vibrated again, and she read Amanda's message. *I wish you were moving here. Maybe one day?*

She debated telling Amanda their plans, but she thought better of it. That was Carson's news to break to his family. Another text bubble appeared from Amanda.

Oops, my boss is standing over my desk looking hot and sexy. I better go before I get fired. Or punished! Oh, wait…I might like that. Ha ha!

Tawny slipped her phone back into her pocket, happiness blooming inside of her.

When Carson finally joined her, she was at the head of the line. "Sorry that took so long, babe."

"Carson, if you need to go into the office, it's fine. We can go back. I can go through the rest of my dad's things. I really don't mind."

"I've got it under control. I'll swing by the office for an hour early tomorrow morning to sign off on a few things. You can sleep in and I'll be back before you know it."

"Are you sure? You can go in now if you need to."

"Can y'all talk about that some other time or move aside please?" the busty blonde behind them in line asked.

"Sorry," Tawny said, and dragged Carson to the back of the room, where there were numerous racks of costumes. Along the side of the room were several dressing rooms.

"Are we really…?" Carson asked.

"We are *really*." She fingered through a rack and handed two costumes to Carson. Then she grabbed two for herself. "Let's see if you can fit all those muscles of yours in one of those."

He inhaled the tiny telltale breath she loved and grabbed masks from a nearby shelf, flashing a haughty grin. "If we have to do this, it's going to be worth our while."

"Those masks don't go with the costumes." She followed him into a dressing room and set the costumes on the bench. "Thank you for—"

He hauled her against him, capturing her mouth with unexpected passion, kissing her so deeply she grabbed at his chest to combat her wobbly knees. Holy moly, she needed to suggest they dress up in costumes more often! He pushed her coat off her shoulders and began kissing her neck, making her entire body hum.

"Carson," she whispered as he devoured a meal of *neck with a side of earlobe.*

"Yes, beautiful?" He tugged her sweater up above her breasts and pulled the cup of her bra down, enjoying his next course.

She closed her eyes and whispered, "What's gotten into you?"

"You, baby. Always and only you."

He loved her breast so passionately she leaned back against the wall to remain standing.

"*Carson—*"

"Have you ever had sex in a dressing room?" he whispered fast and quiet as he shrugged off his coat and stripped hers off, too. He worked the button on her jeans. "Wait. Don't answer that."

"Of course not," she said with a nervous laugh. *Oh my God! Do I want to?*

Carson kissed her neck, his hands roaming all over her body. It took only a second for her to follow his lead, and though she could hardly believe she was actually doing it, she unbuttoned his jeans as he pushed hers down, and they both stripped them off.

"Then it's a first for both of us," he said as they took off their underwear.

"This isn't exactly a *secure* dressing room. What if we get caught?"

"Shh, baby. The door is locked." He lifted her into his arms, holding her up like she was weightless. "If you mean no, then say it now, baby. I'll put you down, no hard feelings. No pressure."

"We'll smell like sex," she whispered.

"Yes or no, Tabby? It's your call."

She was wet and ready, and so nervous about getting caught she was trembling. But she'd never done anything like this, and a big part of her wanted to chase the high of doing something so risky with Carson. Only with Carson.

"Yes, Carson. Always yes." He lowered her onto his shaft and pivoted his hips, turning her insides to liquid heat. "*Ohmygod.*"

"Shh," he said gently. Using the wall for leverage, he moved at a dizzying pace, stroking over all her best spots. "*Be* with me, baby. Let everything else go."

"Was this my surprise?"

He chuckled. "No. I thought we'd look through the comics. We were having so much fun, and we've gotten so close, I just can't resist you."

"Is this another one of your tests? Because—" *Good Lord, you feel good. If this is a test, I want to be a straight A student.* She tried to concentrate past the delicious sensations, and abandoned the idea of convincing him—or herself—that this was a bad idea.

"If we get caught," she said halfheartedly, "I'm going to kill you."

"It's not a test, baby. I *want you* this badly, but if you keep talking we *will* get caught."

He lowered his mouth to hers. The scent of sex and the undeniable aroma of secret thrills hovered around them. She clung to his shoulders, imagining people on the other side of the door sniffing the air. But she knew her olfactory senses were far better than the average person's, and she told herself no one else would notice. She dug her fingers into his shoulders, unable to keep from greedily meeting his efforts despite her worries.

"You can't come inside me," she panted out. "I have wet wipes in my purse, but it's still too messy."

He stilled. "Where do you suggest I…?"

She licked her lips, and his eyes went volcanic. He buried his face in her shoulder.

"Christ, baby. You better come quick. Just knowing you want me in your mouth almost made me lose it."

"Quick? I'm worried they're going to catch us. I don't think I can come at all. Maybe we should just take care of y—"

He slid one hand between them, teasing her most sensitive nerves and sending a tornado of ice and heat soaring through her. She slammed her eyes shut, and must have made a noise because Carson silenced her with another urgent kiss. The fear of being caught brought a whole new level of anxiety—and excitement. She felt vulnerable and *alive.* Her heart raced, and somehow every touch was even more exhilarating. She pushed her hands into his hair, reveling in its soft familiarity and in the trust and safety of *him.* He broke their kiss, whispering sweetnesses into her ear and pushing the rest of the world away.

They were so connected, so utterly in sync in every way, she felt herself slipping away, and in the next second, thunderous waves of ecstasy consumed her.

Carson held her tighter, whispered roughly. "That's my girl. I've got you, Tabby."

His voice propelled her higher, and when he kissed her again, it was a kiss of promises, a safe, *thankful* kiss. When she went slack as a rag doll, he grabbed the base of his cock, and she knew he was on the verge of losing it. He helped her down, and he barely made it into her mouth before the first warm, salty jet hit the back of her throat. He fisted his hand in her hair, gritting his teeth through his release. It sent prickles of heat skating over her skin, making her want to come again and again. When he had nothing left to give, he lifted her to her feet and kissed her breathless.

"You almost done in there?" a man called through the door.

Tawny clung to Carson as he calmly stepped in front of her—a barrier between her and the stranger.

"Just a few more minutes," Carson said in an authoritative voice that vibrated through her. He lifted her chin and kissed her with tenderness that defied his tone.

He was steady. Calm.

And he'd just convinced her to have sex in a public place.

Holy. Shit.

Chapter Fifteen

MUCH MORE THAN a few minutes later, they paid for their costumes and ran down the street toward the hotel, laughing and clinging to each other. Carson felt ridiculous dressed as Ronon Dex from *Stargate Atlantis* in a pair of distressed leather pants and vest, wrist cuffs, and a Chewbacca mask, while Tawny looked like she was made for her Harley Quinn costume, although the alien mask didn't quite go. He obviously hadn't been paying close enough attention when he'd grabbed the masks, but they did the trick.

"Thank heavens for wet wipes," Tawny said. "You just put all my fears to the test."

"You could have told me *no*."

"That's like telling a crack addict, 'Just say no.'" She laughed, and they both took off their masks and put them in the bag.

"Hey, at least I thought to grab masks. I knew if we got down and dirty you'd want a way to escape the store without being recognizable."

"*So* thoughtful." She cuddled up to him as they waited to cross the street. "I still can't believe you got me to do that."

"What can I say? I can't keep my hands off of you."

"Are you into public sex? Was that just the beginning?" she asked in a voice thick with worry as they crossed the street.

When they reached the sidewalk, he stopped walking and took her by the shoulders, gazing into her eyes. "No. I'm *not*, and it wasn't the beginning of anything. I'm sorry. I'm not sure what came over me. I've never done anything like that before, but I thought about the commitment we'd just made and..." He gathered her in his arms and kissed her softly. "I'm so in love with you, Tawny, it just happened. I'll never ask you to do something like that again. I was just as nervous as you were."

"It's not like you forced me into doing it, Carson. I wanted to. But you definitely hide your nervousness a lot better than I do."

He draped an arm around her, walking toward the hotel to get her out of the cold. "My inner voice was saying, 'Holy shit, she's going to let me do this!'" He laughed, and she swatted him, her laughter filling the air.

"I thought you were so calm, cool, and collected."

"Nervous as hell." He kissed her again. "Told you we were perfect for each other."

Inside the hotel, people of all ages were milling about, dressed up like science fiction characters. Carson still felt ridiculous in his costume, but the smile on Tawny's face was worth it. They walked around the banquet rooms checking out artists and new comic books by emerging authors. Tawny pointed out costumes and chatted with vendors and other festival goers. A bright-eyed little girl also dressed up as Harley Quinn patted Tawny's hand.

"Oh my! Look at you!" Tawny's smile reached her eyes as she crouched beside the little girl. "Are you the real Harley Quinn? If so, can I have your autograph?"

The little girl giggled. "I'm not. It's a costume! I'm not even old enough to see the movie!"

"Well, it's spectacular."

The little girl's mother, who was dressed up as Wonder Woman, asked if she could take a picture of the two of them. Tawny touched the side of her head to the child's, beaming like she'd never been happier.

Carson took a few pictures with his phone. As he looked at Tawny through his phone's lens, he wondered what kind of magic had to happen in order for two people to find each other after so many years had passed. His mother's words came back to him. *Sometimes all the rational thinking in the world won't get you what you need. It takes a little magic.*

"Thank you," the little girl's mother said to Tawny, pulling Carson from his thoughts.

"Would you mind taking a picture of me and my girl-friend?" he asked.

"Sure."

Carson handed her his phone and wrapped his arm around Tawny's waist. After she took several pictures and returned his phone, he texted them to Tawny, and they went to watch a costume contest happening in another room.

"I can't believe you wanted a picture after griping about wearing a costume."

"I figured you might want to show them to Adeline." He leaned in for a kiss and said, "It might be the only time you get to see me in a costume."

"That was so thoughtful, thank you. She's more of a pink bows and lace type of girl, but I think she'll get a kick out of them." Her gaze slid down his body. "And now that I know how good you look in leather pants, I might have to fill my bedroom with costumes."

"There's my naughty girl."

"I wonder if there's a Chris Hemsworth costume?"

"You mean Thor?" he asked.

"No, actually, I meant Chris."

He grabbed her ribs, and she spun around, laughing as she dodged a crowd of people dressed up like the crew of Star Trek. He caught up to her in two strides and hauled her against him.

"I don't share," he said in the sternest voice he could, but she was so damn adorable, laughing and flashing that smile. *Christ.* That smile undid him, and he had to laugh.

She waggled her brows. "How about Chris Evans?"

"Captain America," he growled.

She wound her arms around his neck and went up on her toes. "You're very hot when you're jealous. Can I call you Ronon tonight?"

How can I be jealous of a frigging guy behind a costume? "We are definitely going to have a problem if you call me some other guy's name. No more costumes for you."

"Darn it. I was thinking you might enjoy me dressed up as the chick in *Blade Runner*, but if you'd rather not—"

"Wait," he said, picturing her nearly naked, with a few strategically placed pieces of fabric and sparkles all over her body. "Let's negotiate."

THEY GRABBED DINNER in the hotel, poring over the dozens of pictures they'd ended up taking throughout the afternoon and evening, and when they watched the movie, they snuggled and held hands. Carson must have kissed Tawny a hundred times, whispering sweet, important things that told her how serious he was about them, like, *We'll do more of this*

together and *Are you allowed to take Adeline out? We could take her to see Beauty and the Beast.* She didn't think it was possible to fall any harder for him than she already had, but the way he'd begun including Adeline simply because he knew she was important to her brought a sense of bottomless joy.

After the movie, they changed out of their costumes, and when Tawny came out of the hotel restroom she found Carson standing with his back to her at the end of the hall, his phone pressed to his ear. She waited for him to finish his call before joining him. He wrapped her in his arms, his face serious again.

"The time's going by too fast, Tabs. You're leaving tomorrow."

A lump rose in her throat. "I know. I don't want tonight to end."

"I'm coming with you. I'll stay for a few weeks, meet Adeline. We can figure out if you want to open your business. I don't care what we do. I'm not ready to be without you again."

She tried to swallow past the lump, but it swelled, allowing only a tight inhalation to pass. Blinking against damp eyes, she forced her words to come. "Your work?"

"I've got it under control," he assured her. "Your flight was booked, so I've made arrangements to use the company jet. We'll leave at the same time as your original flight, around four."

Her heart beat so fast she could barely catch her breath. "You can do that? So fast?"

"It's done, baby. Unless you have an issue with it?"

"Are you kidding?" Her costume dropped from her hands and she leaped into his arms. "I can't believe it! You're coming with me! You mean for now, right?" She was thrilled that they'd have more time, but she didn't expect him to move there.

"For now, yes. However long *now* is. I can't be without you, baby."

She kissed him again and again, her head spinning. "I didn't know how I would survive leaving half my heart here with you."

"Now you won't have to."

Chapter Sixteen

CARSON STARTLED AWAKE and reached for Tawny, finding an empty space. His gaze darted around the room. The bathroom light was off. He bolted from bed, pulled on a pair of briefs, and headed downstairs. "Tabs?"

He found her sitting on the floor in front of the recliner, wearing the college sweatshirt he'd given her during that snowstorm way back when. The reading light beside the chair cast a glow around her. She looked up from the pile of letters in her lap with tears in her eyes, a sorrowful smile on her lips.

"Baby, what's the matter?" He crossed the room and sat beside her, wiping away her tears.

"I woke up and realized I hadn't finished going through the boxes. I'm sorry if I woke you."

"You didn't. Are the letters sad?"

She shook her head. "No. I mean, some are kind of sad, but my parents had the most beautiful relationship. My mom was funny and flirty. My dad told me she was, but it's different seeing it in her own words. I wonder if I would have been like that if she hadn't died."

"Baby, you are funny and flirty. I love who you are."

"But she sounds like she was so comfortable with herself. In the letters, she tells my father about parties she went to and how she wished he was there. I've always been like my dad, reserved and careful. I just wish I had gotten a chance to know her."

More tears slid down her cheeks. He wrapped her in his arms and pressed a kiss to her forehead.

"I'm sorry you never had that chance to know her better, but I love your reserved, careful side as much as I adore your fun, flirty side. I was drawn to you from the very first time you looked at me from behind your beautiful long hair. And when you set those big green eyes on me, looking at me like I was your worst nightmare? Like, 'what the hell could this big dumb guy know about anything?'"

She laughed.

"You had me at that very moment, Tabs. And the first time I heard that nervous laugh? Babe, my insides went all squirrely. And when you spoke, and all that quiet intelligence came out, my whole being came to life. Suddenly this beautiful, nervous, brilliant girl was my study partner, and she was the most adorably sexy person I'd ever seen. You were so far out of my league." He brushed his thumb over her cheek, cradling her jaw as he'd done a million times and he knew he'd do a million more. "And then you were mine. You were right there with me nearly every night of the week, and for the first time in my life, I was afraid to make a move."

"You were *not*."

"Tabs?" he said flatly. "Did I make a move on you even once before that party? Did I try to kiss you? Touch you?"

"No..."

"I needed those drinks as much as you did the night of the party. Like I said, we're perfect for each other."

"I never would have guessed." She glanced down at the letter again and used the sleeve of the sweatshirt to wipe her tears.

"I see you kept my sweatshirt," he said, hoping to lighten the mood.

"Of course I kept it. It was in the box. I didn't think Keith would appreciate it." She waved the letters. "My parents' relationship reminds me of us. When they finally realized they were a couple, the tone of the letters changed. Were we like that? When we went from friends to lovers, before I freaked out, did my tone change? Do you remember?"

"Yeah. I remember." He tucked her hair behind her ear so he could see her face more clearly. "I remember thinking you looked at me differently, and *knowing* I looked at you like I wanted you. I couldn't sit close to you without getting turned on, and you always ended up snuggled beside me. I basically went through college sporting wood because of you."

She laughed. "Some part of me *really* likes knowing that."

He lifted her hand to his lips and kissed her knuckles. "But it was more than that, Tabs. I was sleeping with my best friend. You made me realize that sex was more than just something that made me feel good. We laughed, and teased. We were so volcanic. I don't know how we survived it. I didn't know it then, but while you were struggling with all those sexual urges, I was falling in love with you." He tipped her chin up and kissed her. "That love has never gone away, and now it's ten times as strong."

"For me, too," she said. From beneath the stack of letters she withdrew a leather-bound journal and handed it to him.

"What's this?"

"They're letters I wrote to you and never sent." She leaned her head against his shoulder.

"We were together four or five nights a week, and you wrote me letters?"

"Mm-hm. There aren't that many, really, and some are more like diary entries than letters. I wrote on and off throughout college, and after graduation, when we were broken up, I kept writing. But I stopped when I started dating Keith. I had to try to move on." She sighed, a small smile lifting her lips. "*Try* being the operative word."

"Are you sure you want me to read them?" he asked, feeling like he was invading her privacy.

"I think you should. I ended things once, and I know I hurt you as badly as I hurt myself. It was the biggest mistake of my life. I know I won't do it again, but I want you to know in your heart that I've always been yours. I don't want you to have any questions about my love for you, and I think the only way for you to be one hundred percent certain is to know what I was feeling."

"Tabs, I trust you. You have nothing to prove to me, and you never will."

Her gaze dropped to the journal and then to the letters in her hand that her mother had written. "I'm learning so much about my parents through these letters. Read them. Please?"

He opened the journal as Tawny turned back to the letters from her mother.

Carson, I wonder if it's wrong to have feelings for you. In just a few short weeks you've become my best friend, but I want so much more. You bring out a fun side of me I never knew existed. When you text, my heart leaps, and I know it shouldn't. I could never handle being one of your many women, and I don't want to ruin our friendship.

He paused to process what he'd read before reading several more notes, each word burrowing into his heart.

Carson, how am I supposed to handle the way you touch my face or push my hair out of my eyes when we're studying? Your touches feel intimate. Do you know I cling to every one of them, hoping that one day we might be more?

He could have written the same words to her back then. He pulled Tawny closer as she picked up another letter and he read the next few entries, stopping cold at the one dated just a week before they started sleeping together.

They say when you fall in love you see fireworks or hear angels sing, but I think they're wrong. I don't see or hear those things. I tried so hard not to fall in love with you that all I heard was a voice in my head telling me not to screw up our friendship. But I guess we both know chemistry is more powerful than the human mind. I fell in love with your scent, the sound of your confident steps on your dorm room floor, the touch of your hand on my skin. I fell in love with the way you say my name—like a bird soaring through the sky, strong and fluid, then disappearing out of sight, soft and ethereal. I fell in love with your analytical mind and the way your brows knit when you're thinking. And that tiny breath you take right before you make a decision. You probably don't realize you do it, but for a few seconds I hold my breath until it comes, and then it fills me so completely, I know this is love.

He pressed a kiss to Tawny's head as she picked up another of her mother's letters and began reading. How could he have been so blind back then? They'd lost so much time.

Turning back to the journal, he read about their sexual relationship, feeling like a voyeur.

Who is this person you've awakened in me? I'm the quiet girl, the smart, careful one. I'm definitely not a sexy, confident vixen, but when we're together, that's the person I become, and somehow I know it's the person I'm supposed to be—with you. Only with you, Carson. What we do feels right and comes naturally. I never knew two people could be so close and yet so far apart. I wish for so many things. A real relationship with you, one where there's only you and me, and where my shyness wouldn't hold you back from going out and doing all the things you love to do with your friends. But I know that can never be.

He skipped ahead, having a hard time reliving the years of wanting something he didn't think he could ever really have while knowing that he could have had it. He gazed down at the page dated right before she'd ended things between them, and his stomach knotted.

I don't understand what's happening to me, but thoughts of you, of us, of what we do together, have become an ominous shadow to my every move. I can't even pay attention in class anymore. I'm full of hope and fear and you, Carson. I'm so full of YOU. What is that? I'm worried your friends know about what we do, or that my friends will find out. What will they think of me? "Chemistry Student by Day, Sexual Vixen by Night." I'm so confused. I want you and I love what we do together. What does that make me? What does it mean? I feel the fear of being exposed pulling me away, and at the same time, when we're together I'm drawn deeper into us. I'm scared, Carson, and the only time I'm not is when I'm in your arms. I know that's not healthy, but it's true.

His heart couldn't take much more. He turned to the last page, her careful cursive writing staring back at him.

It's been twenty-three days since I was in your arms. Seventeen days since we graduated and since I've seen my best friend. Do you know how easy it is to miss you? I hear your voice as I drift off to sleep. I see your face in my dreams. I can't shake the feeling of your hands on my body, and I don't want to. But I know I have to. Goodbye, Carson.

AFTER READING HER mother's letters and feeling the impact of her mother's own words deepening her connection, Tawny knew that when Carson read her feelings they would have a different effect on him than just hearing about them. And she felt him grow tense with every word he read. But he was making such big, life-altering decisions to be with her. She wanted to be sure he knew exactly how deep her love for him went.

He closed the journal and set it aside. His pained and watchful gaze searched her face, reaching for her thoughts. She set the last few unopened letters on the floor and crawled into his lap, straddling him so they were forced to face each other. She felt as raw and exposed as an open wound and saw that she'd caused the same pain in him. All wounds needed fresh air to heal, and this one was no different.

His arms circled her, his hands spreading across her back possessively. "Do you resent me?"

"What?" The question was so far out of the realm of what she'd expected, it took her a moment to form a response. "No, I don't resent you. I love you, Carson. If we'd never met, I could have gone my whole life never knowing what true love was."

"But, Tabs. I hurt you. I made you confused and scared."

"You didn't do either of those things. They were *my* issues caused by my naïveté. It was my learning curve to deal with and figure out who I was as a woman." She gazed down at the necklace she'd given him, the *h* shining against his chest, and felt herself smiling. "I see it this way. You know how sometimes kids are born with a feature that looks too big, like a nose or eyes, and people say they'll grow into it?"

He nodded.

"That's how I think of us. Our love was too big. We had to grow into it." She touched his cheeks, the pain in his eyes tearing at her. "Did I make a mistake asking you to read them?"

"No, babe. You were right. I understand even more clearly exactly what you went through. But it hurts. I hate knowing you were so confused, and the reality of it is that a few conversations back then could have helped. That's the part that kills me. We could have saved each other so much pain if I hadn't given you the space you asked for."

"Or if I had been brave enough to tell you the truth," she said. "We're both at fault, Carson, for the good and the hurtful. But I'm here now, and I'm yours if you still want me. I'm done running."

"Nothing will ever make me stop wanting you."

Chapter Seventeen

THE NEXT MORNING after Carson left for work, Tawny made breakfast, remembering how they couldn't keep their hands off each other their first morning together. It felt like she'd been there for a month, not just shy of a week. She showered and dressed in her skinny jeans, which went so well with the boots Carson had given her. She put on a white blouse with a scalloped lace hem and a wide collar, giving Carson easy access to her shoulders. She put on her most comfortable long cardigan, her favorite because it was soft, had big pockets, and was speckled with pink, black, and white. She felt pretty, and when she looked in the mirror, her eyes were brighter than they had been in years. She looked *happy*. Even her skin looked more radiant than it had before, and she couldn't seem to stop smiling. When Tiffany called to say goodbye, she said she could hear the smile in Tawny's voice. They talked for half an hour about the possibility of opening her own perfumery, which was another thing she couldn't stop thinking about. This morning she and Carson had talked about it again, and they'd begun making a list of the things she'd need in order to move forward. It was beginning to feel real. *Almost as real as my relationship with Carson.*

Ally texted a few minutes later, making Tawny feel like she already had a circle of friends. *Have a safe trip and let me know when you come back so we can get together. I'll torture you with yoga!*

Yoga didn't sound like torture to Tawny, especially if she was doing it with the girls. She sent her a quick reply before packing her bags. *Thank you. I'll look forward to it. I'm glad we had a chance to meet.*

Even though Carson was going with her to Paris, filling her suitcase brought a sense of finality. Tomorrow they'd be in *her* apartment, in *her* world. A world that had felt lonely for more years than not, and now felt full to near bursting. She had the urge to call her father and tell him how happy she was. When he'd first died, she'd reached for the phone on a weekly basis for about a month, wanting to touch base, to hear his voice. She rarely felt that familiar urge anymore, and she realized it was because until now, with the exception of the time she spent with Adeline, she hadn't had many things happen in her life worth sharing. It was funny how one question could change a person's direction in life so dramatically.

She headed downstairs, scrolling through the pictures of her father on her phone. He had been the epitome of a scientist, with wire-framed glasses, blondish hair that was always sticking up, and clothes that were never pressed, as if he'd just rolled out of bed, or had been up for days working. She found her favorite picture of him, taken two Christmases before he died. He hadn't lost weight yet, and still looked healthy. He was reaching up to put the angel on top of the tree, and he'd turned when she'd called his name—"Dad?" His brows were lifted, and a hint of a smile played on his unshaven face. His dress shirt was untucked on one side, rumpled, and it had an ink stain on the pocket. Her heart ached to hear him say, "What is it, Tawn?" He'd hardly ever called her Tawny, as if his mind moved on to the next thought too fast for his mouth.

She stood by the mantel and ran her finger over the picture of her father's handsome face. "Thanks, Dad," she said softly. *Now when I look in the mirror, I see happiness and love and all the things that were missing. I can honestly say I only have a few regrets.* Everyone had a few, didn't they? She regretted ending things with Carson in college instead of having the courage to talk things out, and she regretted her visit to the BDSM club, which was horrendously mortifying. She also regretted marrying Keith when she hadn't been truly in love with him. That hadn't been fair to either of them. But at least now she wasn't carrying her biggest regret of all—hiding her feelings from Carson and trying to live without him.

She looked over the pictures on the mantel and walked around the room touching the back of the couch, the balcony doors, the recliner. She was comfortable there. More comfortable than she was in her own apartment in Paris. Was it Carson? Would her apartment feel more like a home with him there?

She sat down in front of the recliner and set her phone on the floor to leaf through the last few letters she hadn't yet read. The first was sent five months before her mother was killed. She set it aside, examining the second envelope, sent two months later. She wanted to read them, but she also wanted to savor them. She put that one with the other and her jaw dropped open at the sight of her name scrawled across the last envelope—in her father's handwriting. He must have known she'd go through her mother's letters after all.

She swallowed tightly and opened the stiff envelope, withdrawing a photograph of her and Carson in their first year of college. They were so young. His arms and chest weren't nearly as strong as they were now. His face still held the softer sheen of a teen on the cusp of manhood. The picture was taken the night they'd had dinner with her father. They were sitting side by side at the table, gazing deeply into each other's eyes like lovers, though they had only been friends at the time. She remembered that evening and her father asking if he could take their picture. As he'd dug out his camera, he'd asked, "Why aren't *you two* dating?" They'd only looked at each other for a second or two before laughing at the question and facing the camera. How had he captured that moment so perfectly? How had *she* missed the way Carson had looked at her?

She turned the picture over, finding her father's messy handwriting. It was as illegible to most people as a physician's, but Tawny had always been able to decipher his scribbles. She read what he'd written. *When you don't know the answer, question the question.* He'd known all along? He'd seen through their veil of friendship? A veil neither of them had the guts to breach for two long years.

She was sitting in the recliner reading her mother's letters and soaking in every overly exuberant exclamation point when the front door opened and Carson walked in. Holy cow. His chiseled jaw line had a sheen of dark whiskers, making his lips appear even fuller and more kissable as they curved up in an appreciative smile, and he closed the gap between them. His leather bomber jacket made him look even bigger and broader than he was. He looked like the sexiest badass genius she'd ever seen. The necklace she'd given him glimmered against a patch of dark chest hair between the open buttons of his dress shirt.

"How's my beautiful girl?" He leaned down for a kiss, bringing his intoxicating sandalwood and champagne scent.

"Mm. I would like to breathe you in all day long."

His warm lips touched hers again. "That can be arranged.

But first we have someplace we need to go." He pulled her to her feet, his gaze raking down the length of her. "You look good enough to eat."

Would she ever get used to his naughty talk? She bit her lower lip, and he tugged it free with his teeth.

"If we don't leave, I'm going to be all over you."

"Not a threat," she whispered.

He chuckled and helped her on with her coat. They headed out to the car, where Barton was waiting.

Tawny gazed out the window, feeling the heat of Carson's stare like a sunburn, rousing a nest of butterflies in her stomach. When she met his gaze, he had *that* look on his face. The one that told her that all the feelings she felt were real. "Why are we rushing? I thought we weren't meeting Mick for another hour."

"We're not, but I have a surprise for you."

"The last time you surprised me, we ended up having sex in a dressing room."

He brushed his grinning lips over hers. "An act of passion. If I didn't love you so much, maybe it wouldn't be an issue."

"Then I hope you try to have sex in public with me for the next hundred years."

He raised his brows with a look that told her he was happy to comply.

"I said 'try.' You won't succeed."

A few minutes later Carson squeezed her hand and said, "Close your eyes, Tabs."

"What? Why?"

"Because," Carson said in a low voice, "you trust me enough to do what I ask."

She swallowed hard. *That probably shouldn't turn me on, but it does.* She closed her eyes, and the car came to a stop. She felt the warmth of Carson's face near hers, smelled his minty breath. The car door opened and cold air rushed in. She felt Carson's retreat before she heard him step from the car, and then his hand was on hers, helping her onto the sidewalk. His other hand settled on her lower back, firm and protective, as he led her silently along the sidewalk. Surrounded by the scents of the city—exhaust, fried foods, and a plethora of indistinguishable human smells—she heard the bustle of people passing by, felt them encroaching on her personal space, and clung a little tighter to Carson.

"I've got you, babe." They stopped walking. "I'm going to take my hands off you, but you're fine. Nobody's going to run into you. Keep your eyes closed, please."

She heard the *clink* of keys, the *whoosh* of a door. Carson's hand touched her back, guiding her forward. The sweet scent of roses engulfed her, and Carson's hands left her again, followed by the sound of keys and a lock latching.

"Carson…?" Her heart beat a mile a minute.

"Open your eyes, Tabs."

Her gaze coasted over a sea of red roses covering every inch of the floor and countertop in what was once the Biology Café. "Carson? I don't understand."

"I made a few calls and found out the café shut down three months ago. The building was for sale. Now it's yours. I close on it next month."

Tears sprang to her eyes. "I…but…You bought it? For me?"

Carson stepped in front of her and took her hand in his. "I know we're going to Paris, and that's still the plan. I don't want you to leave Adeline. But you're my forever, baby. I want your dreams to come true, and I want to be there to help you and celebrate with you, whether it's here or in Paris, or anywhere else you want to live. I know how much this place means to you, and now it'll never be taken away. There's no pressure to do anything with it. If you ever want to open your business here—next year, in five years, *ten*—it'll be waiting for you."

A river of tears slid down her cheeks. "Oh, Carson. This is *so* much."

"Too much?" He arched a brow. "If you say yes, know I'm going to tell you to get used to it." He smiled, and a nervous laugh escaped her lips. He framed her face with his hands, holding her gaze. "I let you go once. I'm never letting you go again, baby."

He dropped to one knee, and her hands flew to her gaping mouth, dams to her falling tears. *Ohmygod...*

"Tawny Faith Bishop, I have loved you for so many years, I don't know what life would be like without loving you. You're a part of me, and for as long as I live, I want you by my side. I want to love you, cherish you, and see that sparkle in your eyes every day of our lives. I promise to take you to a real Comic Con, and we won't have sex in public places—"

Another nervous laugh fell from her lips.

He rose to his feet, big and broad, and she swore she felt his loving, open heart beating between them. He pulled out a box from the inside pocket of his coat and withdrew a gorgeous ring with two infinity-twisted rose-gold bands with inlaid diamonds, connected by a marquis-cut diamond. One band only went three-quarters of the way around, ending at the stunning diamond, forming the letter *h*.

"Marry me, Tabby. Be my *constant*, and I promise to make the rest of our lives better than you ever dreamed possible. Will you be my wife, baby?"

She opened her mouth to speak, and sobs burst out. It was

all she could do to throw her arms around his neck, nodding like a bobblehead doll. He twirled her around, his deep, sexy laugh making her laugh, too. When he set her feet back on the ground, he put the gorgeous ring on her finger and brushed his thumb over the back of her hand.

"You should probably say yes," he said, drawing more elated laughter and tears.

"Yes, Carson. Yes! A million times around the earth and back. *Yes!*"

Chapter Eighteen

"I CAN'T STOP smiling, or looking at the ring," Tawny said as they rode the elevator up to Mick's office. "How did you get a ring like this made this so fast?"

While she was busy admiring her new engagement ring, Carson hadn't been able to take his eyes off his new *fiancée*. "I had it made after you gave me this." He touched the necklace she'd given him. "My friend Sterling Silver, the jeweler I told you about, who works in the same way you hope to, made it. And yes, that's his *real*, given name." He drew her against him, drinking in her contagious smile. "You didn't think I'd get my Tabs a generic engagement ring, did you?"

"I didn't *think*." She laughed. "Carson, a week ago I was wondering if you were married, or if you'd even remember me, and now..."

"Now we're doing what we should have done a decade ago. I love you, Tabs, and nothing will ever take that away."

The elevator opened, and Carson draped an arm over Tawny's shoulder as they approached the receptionist, Hilary, a fortysomething brunette who had worked for Mick for several years. "Hi, Hilary. How are you?"

"Just fine, Carson," she said, eyeing Tawny with a friendly, and curious, smile. "And you?"

"Marvelous, thank you." He gazed at Tawny, knowing he

was wearing his heart on his sleeve, and proud of it. "Tawny, this is Hilary. Hilary, this is my fiancée, Tawny Bishop." *Fiancée.* He liked the sound of that.

Tawny's eyes sparkled with the introduction, and her gorgeous smile got even brighter. "Hi. It's nice to meet you."

The surprise in Hilary's expression did not go unnoticed as she rose to her feet and came around the desk. She had forever nagged Carson about letting her introduce him to women.

"Carson Bad, you little devil. Where have you been hiding this beautiful woman?" Hilary embraced him. Then she turned to Tawny and hugged her, too. "Congratulations to you both. Three Bad boys down. Now if we could only get Brett to see the forest through the trees, maybe he'd settle down and finally ask out Sophie."

Carson laughed. "I'm not sure I'd wish that on Soph." He was only kidding. Brett was a smart-ass, and he could be pompous, but Carson knew that beneath it all his brother was as loyal as the rest of them. But that didn't mean it wasn't fun keeping his reputation alive.

"Go on back. Mick should be in his office," Hilary said. "And congratulations again."

Sophie met them on their way down the hall. "Hi, Carson. And you must be Tawny. Amanda told me you'd be coming by. It's so nice to meet you. I'm Sophie, Mick's assistant."

"It's nice to meet you, too," Tawny said.

Sophie glanced at Tawny's ring, the question in her eyes catching Carson's attention.

"Tawny and I just got engaged."

The pride in his voice was drowned out by Sophie's squeal as she launched herself into his arms. "Congratulations! Oh my goodness! Does Mick know?" She hugged Tawny. "I'm so happy for you. Carson is such a special person. You two make a beautiful couple, and his family is amazing. Oh my gosh. I'm babbling, and I'm not even the one who's engaged."

Tawny laughed. "If I wasn't nervous about meeting Mick, I'd be babbling too."

"I can see how this introduction is going to go." Carson laced his fingers with Tawny. "Shall we go tell Amanda before Soph puts it on the intercom?"

"Oh, good idea," Sophie teased. "I have to go to the file room, but Mick's expecting you."

"Tabs, are you okay?" he asked as they headed for Mick's office. "Is this overwhelming?"

"Yes, I'm okay, and yes, it's overwhelming. But it's supposed to be, right?"

"I guess. It's a bit overwhelming for me, too," he admitted. "In the very best way, of course." He motioned down the hall to Amanda, who was getting up from behind her desk. "Incoming," he said into Tawny's ear.

"Hi! I have been waiting like an expectant mother," Amanda said. "I can't believe you guys are leaving today. Mick said you're going, too, Carson? I knew you would. No man looks at a woman like you look at Tawny and lets her get away."

"*Christ*," he uttered. "Am I that transparent?"

Tawny snuggled into his side. "I think we both are."

"You can't hide love," Amanda said as she led them toward Mick's office.

Love. Carson hadn't thought about that word for years, and ever since Tawny came back, it's all he could think about.

"Amanda." Carson held up Tawny's left hand.

She squealed as loud as Sophie had and threw herself into Tawny's arms. "Oh my gosh! Congratulations! Now we'll really be sisters!"

After another round of hugs and congratulations, they made it to Mick's office.

Mick stood with his back to the door, talking on the phone. He turned, holding up one finger, and motioned toward the chairs. His gaze fell to Tawny, and his brows drew into a serious slant. Carson felt her go rigid beside him. The blood drained from her face, her gaze locked on Mick.

"Tabs?" Carson shot a look at Mick, who was ending his call. His gut twisted as Tawny took a step backward.

"Are you okay?" Amanda asked.

"I feel sick." Tawny turned toward the door, her body trembling. "Bathroom?"

Amanda put an arm around Tawny's waist. "I'll take her."

"I'm com—"

Mick grabbed Carson's arm, holding him back as Amanda and Tawny disappeared out the door. Mick looked the most like their father, with squared-off features and eyes that could cut right through a person, as they were doing now. "Give her a minute."

"What the fuck just happened?" Carson demanded as his brother closed the office door.

"Calm down, Carson. Whatever you're thinking, I'm sure it's wrong."

Carson went for the door, and Mick blocked his way. "What the fuck, Mick? My fiancée just took one look at you and she went from being elated to panic-stricken."

"Fiancée?" Mick scrubbed a hand down his face.

"Yes. I asked her to marry me. Now step out of the way or I swear I'll go through you."

"Damn, Carson. You need to sit down for a minute."

"You got something to say, Mick? Say it." Carson's hands fisted at his sides.

"Where do I start? That's the same girl you were head over heels for in college? Have you spoken to her since? Do you know anything about what she's been up to? I know her, Carson. I met her in Chicago. I didn't know her name, but I went to a club there, and she—"

"Holy hell, Mick. Did you fuck her?" Bile rose in his throat.

"No! *Jesus.* She shouldn't have been there. She was like this scared mouse. I saw her when she came in." Mick paced. "She didn't belong there, and I knew it. I bought her a drink and tried to get her to leave. She was—*is*—beautiful, but she was so scared. Guys eat up girls like that, especially in those exclusive clubs. She wouldn't leave, and I *couldn't* leave. I felt compelled to stick around because she was so out of place. She kept telling me she had to be there, lifting her chin like she was full of courage she didn't have."

Carson's stomach turned over at the thought of *his* Tawny putting herself out there like that because of the things they'd done together. Hearing it from Tawny, and hearing Mick's description of her, brought it slamming into him. He should have pushed harder in college. He never should have let her go.

"Cut to the chase, Mick. I need to go to her."

"It was a BDSM club. She went into a room with a guy, and I was worried, so I stood by, listening. I got her out when things turned out to be more than she could handle. She wouldn't let me drive her home, wouldn't tell me her name. She drove off, and I never saw her again. I had no idea she was *your* Tawny. You're sure she's okay? Stable?"

"I wouldn't marry her if I didn't trust who she was one hundred percent," Carson seethed, out of anger for the situation, for the mortification he knew Tawny must feel. He plowed past Mick and out the office door. "I knew she went to a club," he said under his breath to Mick, who was storming down the hall beside him. "She told me. But I didn't know things went that badly."

He stopped beside the ladies' room, causing Mick to plow into him.

"Thank you for getting her out of there," Carson said. "I love her, Mick. She was there because of things *we* did together in college. She was trying to figure out who she was. It's my fucking fault."

Carson pushed the bathroom door open, and Amanda spun around as he and Mick burst in.

"Where'd she go?" Carson asked.

Amanda pointed to the stall. "She said she's sick, but she won't open up. What should I do?"

"Babe, she'll be okay," Mick said. "Just keep everyone out of the bathroom."

TAWNY PRESSED THE wad of toilet paper to her eyes, trying to stop the flow of tears pouring down her face. Of all the people in the world to have seen her in that stupid, goddamn club, why did it have to be Carson's brother?

"Tabs?" Carson's concerned voice came through the stall door. "It's me, baby. Open up."

She closed her eyes, her heart hurting so badly she could barely think. She tugged at her beautiful engagement ring, her vision blurred from tears. "I know you can't marry me now, but I can't get the ring off. It's stuck."

"Tawny Bishop, if you take that ring off, I will tear this stall apart and tan your sweet ass."

Not a threat. That made her ache even more. Carson was *it* for her. The only man she'd ever want. Her true love. Her one and only.

"Babe, please. I already knew about the club. There's nothing to be embarrassed about."

"Tawny," Mick said.

Her eyes sprang open. Mick was still in the bathroom? *Oh God.*

"I was in that club, too." Mick's deep voice came through the door, closer this time. "We were both there for the same reason. I'm sorry you're embarrassed, but please don't be."

"Oh my God. Not only are my worst fears coming true, but we're at your *brother's* office. Can you two *please* get out of the ladies' room?"

"I'm not leaving until you're in my arms, babe."

"And I'm not leaving until we get past this," Mick declared. "My brother loves you, and there's no way in hell I'm going to walk out that door until this situation is rectified."

"Then we'll be living in the bathroom for a *long* time." She wiped her eyes and crossed her arms over her chest. "Two big men in the women's bathroom. What is your staff going to think? God, I've embarrassed all of us."

"I don't give a rat's ass what his staff thinks, Tabby."

"And I don't get embarrassed," Mick said.

She was silent for a long moment. She loved Carson so much, how could she ever face Mick or Amanda again. "Mick? Does Amanda know?"

"That I used to go to those clubs?" Mick asked. "Yes. I have no secrets from her."

She swallowed hard and forced herself to ask the more difficult question. "Does she...? Did she go to them?" Her voice came out thin and shaky.

"No," Mick answered. "She never has. But the night we first got together, both of us were in costumes and masks. We both thought we were hooking up with a random person in a bar. We almost had anonymous sex in the bathroom. When I realized it was her, I put a stop to it. We've *all* done things that are embarrassing, but that's how we learn and grow as adults."

She'd known this about them—Amanda had told her—but hearing Mick say it made her cry even harder. He didn't hesitate to share his private moment to save his brother's relationship. Brotherly bonds...

"I'm sorry, Carson," she said softly, causing more tears to fall. "I don't even know who the guy was that I was with. What if he was one of your clients and we run into him next month, or next year, or five years from now? How can you ever look at me again?"

Carson's face appeared over the stall door. His concerned, loving gaze sucked the air from her lungs. "Tabby, I wouldn't care if you'd slept with any number of nameless, faceless men before me. I only care that we're together now. You told me the truth, baby. The only part of this that hurts me is that I caused you to search for something you could only find with me. I regret that, and I'll spend the rest of our lives making it up to you."

"It wasn't your fault," she said. "I didn't sleep with that guy. He spoke to me like I was a dog. He wanted me to take off my clothes and sit with my back to him. But he wasn't *you*, and I was petrified to give him control. He got angry and said horrible things, and then Mick came in and he got me out of there." She covered her face. "And I was awful to Mick because I was so embarrassed. And now I'm mortified that I was such a bitch to him and that he saw me there, at the lowest time in my life."

Carson's face disappeared from above the door, and the door crashed open, and then she was in his arms, sobbing into his shirt as he whispered reassurances.

"I'm so sorry," she said.

"It's okay, baby." He pressed a kiss to the top of her head, one hand on her back, the other holding her around her shoulders. Her shield. Her protector. Her best friend. "I've got you, and I am *never* letting go."

Carson's love made her cry harder. What did she do to deserve him? "You're not bothered that Mick knows?"

"Baby, he got you out of a bad situation. As much as I hate him knowing you were in that club because of me, he protected you as if you were his own flesh and blood, and he didn't even know you. I'm not ashamed of you trying to figure out who you were if that's what you're worried about. No. Not even a little." He closed his eyes for a beat, breathing deeply. "We talked about signs before. I think it's a pretty big one that he was there for you."

She tried to focus on Mick through her tears. "I'm sorry, Mick. You must think I'm a slut, but I'm really not. I swear it. There's only been two men since college. My ex-husband and Carson. I've never gone to a place like that except that one time."

"Tawny, I married a woman who thought she was picking up a random guy for a one-night stand," Mick said. "And what's even more remarkable is the fact that the incredible woman standing on the other side of that door married me, a guy who spent years sleeping with women I didn't know. I would never judge you. If anything, I think what you did shows incredible strength in your character. At least you were looking for answers. I was doing everything I could to escape them."

His confession hit her hard. Did everyone have demons they tried to outrun?

Amanda peeked her head into the ladies' room. "Sorry to interrupt, but there's a line forming out here. Are you okay?" Her gaze fell on Tawny.

Oh no. What could she tell her?

"Can you give us another minute, sweetheart?" Mick asked. "Tell them to use the bathroom in my office."

After Amanda closed the door, Tawny said, "How am I ever going to live this down?" What do I tell Amanda? She's been so good to me. I can't lie to her, but what will she think of me if I tell her? How can I marry into your family with this shadowing me?"

"I'm going to leave you two alone to figure this out, but our family has bigger shadows than this, Tawny. This is a blip on the radar screen, even though it feels huge to you right now." Mick reached for the door.

"Wait." Tawny went to him. "I can't ask you to keep a secret from Amanda. I'll tell her." Carson's arm circled her waist, and she drew courage from his support. "If Tiffany can look Brett in the eye after flashing him, I can do this." That earned a smile from each of them, including her.

Mick left the bathroom, and Carson turned her in his arms. "Tiffany told you about flashing us?"

Her tears finally stopped, though her heart was still racing. "Yes."

"Does that mean you'll tell her about this?"

She hadn't thought about that, but now that she was, she

realized she wouldn't feel right keeping a secret with Amanda and not including Tiffany. *If I'm going to be mortified, might as well let everyone in on it.* "Probably."

"Are you okay with that? Do you want to talk about it?"

"No," rushed from her lungs. "I'm so emotionally exhausted, all I want to do is be with you someplace quiet so I can tear apart this nightmare and put it behind me."

He lifted her chin and pressed his lips to hers. "You asked how you could marry into my family with this shadowing you. How can you not?" A tease rose in his eyes.

"Are you questioning my question?"

"I read it on a mug somewhere." He kissed her again. "You scared the hell out of me, baby." He cradled her face in his hands and touched his forehead to hers. "I wish you'd run *to* me—not *away* from me—when you're scared. I'll always be here, and there's no shadow big enough to take me on. My love for you is endless."

"God, I love you," she said, hugging him tight.

"Maybe we should start a new tradition of meeting in this bathroom every year on this date."

She laughed, and it felt so good, it brought more laughter. Slightly hysterical laughter, which led to tears and kisses and more tears—happier tears as her heart put itself back together.

"Ever have sex in a bathroom?" Carson asked between delicious kisses.

"Carson!"

"Can't fault a guy for trying." He took her hand, but she didn't budge.

She was too busy contemplating the lock on the bathroom door.

Epilogue

TAWNY HAD NEVER experienced such a glorious Christmas Eve. The lights of Paris twinkled against the evening sky, shimmering off the falling snow as it blanketed the city. Tawny's gaze drifted from the balcony around her new, large dining room table. The one she'd had wouldn't have allowed for Carson's family and their significant others to join them for their holiday celebration. It was a special night. They'd been granted permission to have Adeline join them for dinner. She and Carson had been visiting her several times each week at the orphanage, and it wouldn't have felt like Christmas without her. She'd immediately taken to his brothers, climbing on them like they were jungle gyms. Mick had been whispering in Amanda's ear all night, and Tawny swore she heard the word *babies* more than once. He was whispering again now. Tiffany, Dylan, and Brett were arguing over who should get the last sweet roll. Tiffany's eye roll told her Brett might win, but she knew if he did, he'd give it to her anyway.

Adeline's giggles drew everyone's attention. She sat on Carson's lap in her pretty new pink taffeta Christmas dress and shiny white Mary Jane's she and Carson had bought her last week when they'd taken her shopping. Carson was busy putting on a very animated puppet show with his napkin, earning more of Adeline's sweet laughter. Tawny had wondered how the two would get along. She'd never seen Carson with a child before, but they'd hit it off from the moment they'd met, and tonight they were inseparable.

Carson's mother, Jackie, tapped Tawny's arm, looking adoringly at the two of them. "If that doesn't make your ovaries explode, I don't know what will."

"I can barely stand it," Tawny admitted. She and Carson had gone to New York for Thanksgiving and had spent several days with his family. His mother had taken Tawny under her wing, treating her as if she were her own daughter. Jackie was funny and insightful, and her love for her children showed in everything she did. Tawny liked to believe her mother would have been the same way.

"Have you guys set a wedding date?" Tiffany asked. She and Dylan had recently gotten engaged, and they were trying to figure out their wedding date just as Carson and Tawny were.

"I wanted to head to Vegas, but Tawny said it wasn't fair to my mom." Carson looked at Adeline. "That's silly, isn't it, Addy girl? Tawny should marry me right this second."

"I'd marry you right this second." Adeline kissed his cheek, and a unified *aw* sounded around the table.

"Vegas?" Jackie sounded appalled. "Baby, you are the last child of mine I'd expect to do something like that. I always thought if any of you did something impetuous, it would be Brett."

Brett sat back with a big grin on his face. "Way to expect great things from me, Mom."

"Oh, honey," Jackie said. "If Lorelei were here, I'd expect her to be impetuous, too. It's that need to live life to the fullest. You were like two peas in a pod that way. It's a *very* good thing."

Carson's family had been sharing their feelings for Lorelei more and more since the fundraiser, and it had continued opening doors between Carson and his father. He'd even called to congratulate Carson on their engagement.

"I can be impetuous," Carson insisted. "Right, Addy girl?"

Adeline smiled up at him. "I don't know what that means, but if it means you can be *red*, then yes. Because you feel red to me."

Adeline put colors together the way Tawny did fragrances. When asked, *What does that taste like?* Adeline would respond with something like, *Kind of blue and a little yellow.* She had no interest in science or computers, or even books. She loved colors and music, especially the piano, which was why there was a new one in their living room. Carson insisted on learning to play, and he was getting pretty good, too.

Carson waggled his brows, and everyone laughed. He hugged Adeline and said, "That's my girl."

Tawny's full life still felt like a dream, but she was no longer afraid she'd wake up alone. Not when there were so many loving family members who refused to be ignored. Tiffany, Amanda, and Ally had all gotten international phone plans and they texted often. She spoke to Jackie once a week on the phone, like she used to do with her father, and she looked forward to those conversations. What she wasn't looking forward to was Carson's return to New York. He was leaving right after the holidays for two weeks to handle business matters, and two weeks felt like forever. She worried about him being so far away from his family and his business, and the truth was, she'd become so attached to his family, she missed them terribly despite the texts and phone calls.

"Tawny's going to make me my own perfume," Adeline

announced to no one in particular. "It's going to smell like flowers and sugar and pink!" She reached up and touched the pink bow on her barrette, which kept her long dark hair out of her eyes.

"That's right, sweet girl." Tawny's heart might explode right along with her ovaries. She had prepared all she could to start her business, but she'd been putting off the final decision about *where* to open it. She wanted to wait until Adeline was adopted by a loving family, and settled, but every day that thought became harder to swallow. Tears sprang to her eyes, and she pushed to her feet and began gathering dishes. "I'll make room for dessert."

"I'll help, Tabs." Carson set Adeline on Jackie's lap.

The others rose to help clear the table.

"You remind me of someone very special," Jackie looked at Adeline adoringly as she tucked the happy little girl's hair behind her shoulders. "Are you ready for Christmas, Miss Adeline?"

"Yes! My Carson and Tawny bought me presents, and there's a party where I live. Can you come? Please?" Adeline had been calling Carson "my Carson" since they met.

She blinked wide baby blues at Jackie, and Tawny swore she saw Jackie melt a little. Her eyes connected with Carson's, and his heart was overflowing with love for them.

He put a hand on Tawny's shoulder and whispered, "Can I talk to you alone for a second?"

"Sure." She followed him into the kitchen and set the dishes down, peeking out at Jackie and Adeline. "They're really getting attached to each other."

His hands cradled her face, and he touched his soft lips to hers, centering her. "You love our little girl."

A single, unstoppable tear slipped down her cheek. "Don't call her that. I think I need to start getting used to the idea of letting her go, or I'll never be able to."

"What if you never had to?" he asked. "What if *we* adopted her, Tabs? She belongs with us. We can get married right away and bring her to the States, where she would have more family than she could ever hope for. You can open your perfumery and work part-time while she's in school."

Tawny couldn't see through her tears, couldn't speak for the thickening of her throat, as her loving fiancé made more of her dreams come true.

"I've wanted to bring it up from the moment I met her, but we had so many pieces of our lives left to figure out, I was waiting for the right time. Having my family here, watching Adeline climb all over Dylan, calling him Dilly, like Lorelei used to do, and swinging from Brett's biceps like a little monkey, reminded me of how life could change in an instant. I'm not willing to take the chance of losing her tomorrow, or the next day, or a year from now. If you want to stay in Paris, we'll do that. But I don't want to let her go, Tabby, and I know you don't either. She's your sign, baby. She's meant to be with us."

With her heart beating wildly and her throat so thick she feared no words would come, Tawny gazed into her best friend's eyes, his endless love consuming her as it always had. She wrapped her arms around his neck, and words did not fail her. "You're wrong, Carson. She's not my sign. She's ours."

Are you ready for Brett Bad?

Indulge your inner vixen with this sexy billionaire!

Meet Brett Bad, the most aggressive and cocky of the Bad brothers. He's fiercely loyal and never accepts no for an answer. It'll take someone stronger than him to tame this Bad boy.

Ready for more Billionaires After Dark?
There are FOUR Wild Boys After Dark books
just waiting to be read.
Meet Logan, Heath, Carson, and Jackson,
and get your steamy love on!

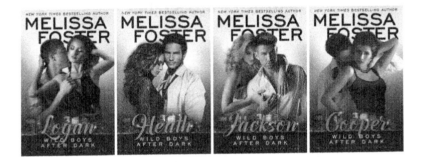

SIGN UP for Melissa's newsletter to stay up to date
with new releases and sales:
www.MelissaFoster.com/Newsletter

More Books By Melissa

BILLIONAIRES AFTER DARK SERIES

WILD BOYS AFTER DARK
Logan
Heath
Jackson
Cooper

BAD BOYS AFTER DARK
Mick
Dylan
Carson
Brett

LOVE IN BLOOM SERIES

SNOW SISTERS
Sisters in Love
Sisters in Bloom
Sisters in White

THE BRADENS at Weston
Lovers at Heart
Destined for Love
Friendship on Fire
Sea of Love
Bursting with Love
Hearts at Play

THE BRADENS at Trusty
Taken by Love

Fated for Love
Romancing My Love
Flirting with Love
Dreaming of Love
Crashing into Love

THE BRADENS at Peaceful Harbor
Healed by Love
Surrender My Love
River of Love
Crushing on Love
Whisper of Love
Thrill of Love

THE BRADEN NOVELLAS
Promise My Love
Our New Love
Daring Her Love
Story of Love

THE REMINGTONS
Game of Love
Stroke of Love
Flames of Love
Slope of Love
Read, Write, Love
Touched by Love

SEASIDE SUMMERS
Seaside Dreams
Seaside Hearts
Seaside Sunsets
Seaside Secrets

Seaside Nights
Seaside Embrace
Seaside Lovers
Seaside Whispers

BAYSIDE SUMMERS
Bayside Desires
Bayside Passions

<u>THE RYDERS</u>
Seized by Love
Claimed by Love
Chased by Love
Rescued by Love

SEXY STANDALONE ROMANCE
Tru Blue
Truly, Madly, Whiskey

<u>HARBORSIDE NIGHTS SERIES</u>
Includes characters from the Love in Bloom series
Catching Cassidy
Discovering Delilah
Tempting Tristan

More Books by Melissa
Chasing Amanda (mystery/suspense)
Come Back to Me (mystery/suspense)
Have No Shame (historical fiction/romance)
Love, Lies & Mystery (3-book bundle)
Megan's Way (literary fiction)
Traces of Kara (psychological thriller)
Where Petals Fall (suspense)

Acknowledgments

I had a blast writing about Carson and Tawny, and I look forward to bringing you Brett Bad's story. If this is your first Bad Boys After Dark novel, Mick and Dylan's books are also available, as well as all four of the Wild Boys After Dark books, and their stories are just as sinfully sexy as Carson's. I hope you'll check out the other series in my big-family romance collection, Love in Bloom, including the Snow Sisters, The Bradens, The Remingtons, Seaside Summers, Bayside Summers, The Ryders, and Harborside Nights. You can find all of my books, publication schedules, reader checklists, and more free reader goodies on my site.

www.MelissaFoster.com

Please keep your emails and your posts on social media coming. If you haven't joined my fan club yet, please do! We have loads of fun, chat about books, and members get special sneak peeks of upcoming publications.

facebook.com/groups/MelissaFosterFans

A special thank-you goes to my incredibly talented editorial team. Thank you, Kristen, Penina, Elaini, Juliette, Marlene, Lynn, and Justinn.

As always, heaps of love and gratitude to my amazing family for allowing me to disappear for hours at a time creating these fictional worlds.

Meet Melissa

www.MelissaFoster.com
www.MelissaFoster.com/Newsletter
www.MelissaFoster.com/Reader-Goodies

Having sold more than three million books, Melissa Foster is a *New York Times* and *USA Today* bestselling and award-winning author. Her books have been recommended by *USA Today's* book blog, *Hagerstown* magazine, *The Patriot*, and several other print venues. She is the founder of the World Literary Café and Fostering Success. Melissa has painted and donated several murals to the Hospital for Sick Children in Washington, DC.

Visit Melissa on her website or chat with her on social media. Melissa enjoys discussing her books with book clubs and reader groups and welcomes an invitation to your event.

Melissa's books are available through most online retailers in paperback and digital formats.

CPSIA information can be obtained
at www.ICGtesting.com
Printed in the USA
BVOW08s0915220617
487587BV00001B/37/P